MEMORIES

"Afraid?" Steven sputtered. "Why should I be afraid?"

"I don't know," Jessica said. "Maybe you're afraid of what people will think about your dating someone new."

Steven got up, his fists clenched in anger. "That's crazy."

"Is it?" Jessica replied. "I think you're terrified of what Betsy will say if you start seeing someone new."

"Jessica!" Elizabeth exclaimed, shocked.

"I don't care what Betsy says," Steven spat out. "I can do whatever I want!"

"Then why do you keep avoiding Cara now, after you've had some good times together?"

Steven slammed his fist on the counter. "I've told you, Jess, stay out of it. I'll live my life the way I want."

"OK," Jessica said. "But remember—Cara's got one advantage over Tricia. She's alive."

Bantam Books in the Sweet Valley High Series
Ask your bookseller for the books you have missed

SWEET VALLEY HIGH

MEMORIES

Written by
Kate William

Created by
FRANCINE PASCAL

BANTAM BOOKS
TORONTO · NEW YORK · LONDON · SYDNEY · AUCKLAND

RL 5, IL age 12 and up

MEMORIES
A Bantam Book / November 1985

ISBN 0-553-25243-7

Published simultaneously in the United States and Canada

Bantam Books are published by Bantam Books, Inc. Its
trademark, consisting of the words "Bantam Books" and the
portrayal of a rooster, is Registered in U.S. Patent and
Trademark Office and in other countries. Marca Registrada.
Bantam Books, Inc., 666 Fifth Avenue, New York, New York
10103.

PRINTED IN THE UNITED STATES OF AMERICA

O   0 9 8 7 6 5 4 3 2 1

MEMORIES

One

"Steven! What's wrong?"

Ned Wakefield looked up from the book he was reading as his son streaked by the master bedroom. Then came the sound of Steven's bedroom door closing with an angry slam.

Alice Wakefield gave her husband a puzzled look. "What do you think could be the matter?"

Ned Wakefield and his eighteen-year-old son were both tall and had the same dark hair and eyes. Right now Mr. Wakefield wore the same troubled expression that Steven had been wearing on and off for weeks. "I don't know," he answered, rubbing his forehead. "Steve has been so much better lately. I was sure he was

1

beginning to let go of Tricia's memory. I hope that's not the problem.''

But that *was* the problem. Steven had forgotten about Tricia Martin, at least for a little while, and now, as he lay staring up at the ceiling of his bedroom, he felt horrible about it. Memories of Tricia, his beautiful girlfriend with her halo of strawberry blond hair and her shining blue eyes, washed over him. Death had taken Tricia from Steven several months ago, but he had vowed always to keep her in his heart.

In spite of his family's love and support, Steven had mourned for weeks following Tricia's death. Lately he had begun to recover from his depression, though Tricia was always in his thoughts. His sister Jessica kept offering to fix him up with dates, and his friends were always telling him he should get out more, but that weekend had been the first time he had felt like being with people.

He had agreed to go to a party that Lila Fowler was throwing. Lila went to school with his twin sisters, Jessica and Elizabeth, at Sweet Valley High. He had called up Tricia's older sister, Betsy, and asked her and her boyfriend, Jason Stone, to come along.

The Fowlers were one of the wealthiest families in Sweet Valley, and any party held at their estate was an event. To his amazement, Steven had actually begun to have a good time. This was

2

not because of the lavish surroundings, but because of Jessica's friend Cara Walker, who had made sure Steven enjoyed himself. Jessica had once fixed up Cara and Steven, and the evening had ended disastrously. Then, the afternoon of the party, Steven had run into Cara and discovered she, too, had been having problems and that she had changed. That night at the party Cara had made Steven relax and smile.

That changed suddenly when Cara and Steven were dancing. Betsy Martin left Jason at the buffet and went up to Steven. Steven and Betsy had been finding comfort in each other's company since Tricia's death, but Betsy's eyes were blazing.

"Having a good time, I see," she commented icily.

"Yeah, it's a nice party," Steven had answered, suddenly feeling uncomfortable.

"I'm surprised at you, Steve," Betsy lashed out, her voice shaking with anger. "I thought you really loved my sister. But the minute another girl starts to look at you, you forget all about Tricia!"

Steven felt as though he had been punched in the stomach. He didn't know how to respond to Betsy's accusation. Before Betsy could say another word, Steven had rushed off the dance floor and raced to his car, without bothering to say goodbye to Cara.

3

Now, lying in the dark, he could see that Betsy had been right. Why should he be out enjoying himself when his beloved Tricia was gone? Tears welled up in Steven's eyes, and he turned his face toward the wall.

I may have betrayed Tricia's memory once, he told himself, *but I will never, ever do it again!*

"So Todd's back in town. No wonder you're wearing that big smile this morning," Mrs. Wakefield teased.

"Yup, we'll have the whole day together," Elizabeth said happily.

Unknown to Elizabeth, Todd Wilkins, her longtime boyfriend, who had moved to Vermont a few weeks earlier, had come back to Sweet Valley to take care of some of his father's unfinished business. Todd had surprised Elizabeth the previous evening by showing up unannounced at Lila Fowler's party. But when Todd had spotted Elizabeth dancing with another boy, he'd assumed she'd forgotten all about their relationship. His feelings crushed, he'd left the party in a hurry. Luckily, Elizabeth had managed to find Todd and clear up the misunderstanding. It was Todd and Todd alone whom she loved. Now Elizabeth was looking forward to the precious hours she and Todd would spend together before he flew home the following morning.

Mrs. Wakefield brought the platter of eggs she had just scrambled to the table and shifted her gaze to Jessica. Even after sixteen years of looking at them, Alice Wakefield was sometimes still surprised at just how identical her pretty twins were. They shared the same sunshine-kissed golden hair and blue-green eyes, and except for a small mole on Elizabeth's right shoulder, their five-foot-six-inch frames were absolutely identical. But the girls' similarities ended with their looks. In personality, they were quite opposite. Elizabeth was calm and steady, while the tempestuous and often conniving Jessica was like a firecracker waiting to go off. Right now her eyes were blazing as she described the previous night's events.

"After Steve got home from the party and went upstairs," Jessica said dramatically, "Lila called to tell me that Betsy Martin made a big scene in front of everyone. She started to yell at Steve for showing too much interest in Cara."

"She did?" Mrs. Wakefield asked with surprise. "That doesn't sound like Betsy."

"I think it sounds exactly like her," Jessica interjected. "You can't get much trashier than Betsy Martin. I don't know why Steve even bothers to talk to her."

"They're friends," Elizabeth answered.

"It's embarrassing," Jessica said distastefully. "I can't believe that girl once stayed in our

5

house. Everyone I know was horrified when they heard one of the Martins was living here."

Jessica was not the only person who had a low opinion of the Martins. Although Sweet Valley was a picture-perfect California town, it did have a bad area, and the Martin family lived there in a ramshackle house. Mr. Martin was known as the town drunk, while Betsy had a reputation for being wild and heavily into drugs. Only Tricia had been able to rise above her family's circumstances. Her illness and death had hit Betsy hard; yet those tragic events had caused Betsy to straighten out her life and win a scholarship to art school in the fall.

When Steven was feeling low, Betsy was often the only person he could bear to be around, and he always seemed happier after they'd spent some time together. The older Wakefields and Elizabeth felt Steven and Betsy gave each other valuable support. But Jessica saw things differently. She thought Betsy Martin was a depressing reminder of her sister and that her friendship was prolonging Steven's misery.

"Where is Steve this morning?" Mr. Wakefield asked, taking a sip of coffee.

"I called him down to breakfast," his wife answered, "but he said he wasn't hungry, so I let him sleep. He really should eat something."

Jessica dropped the slice of toast she was buttering. "I'll go up and get him," she said eagerly.

"I suppose you could give it a try," Mrs. Wakefield said.

"Don't worry, Mom. I'll get him down. He won't be able to resist me," she joked. "No man can." She gave the group a little wink and flounced out of the room.

"Sometimes I wish I had Jessica's attitude toward boys," Elizabeth said, sighing. She stirred some honey into her tea.

"I thought you'd worked things out with Todd," her mother said with concern.

"Oh, we did. It's just so hard for us to be apart." Now that she and Todd were separated, Elizabeth knew what she had to look forward to in the coming months: letters, cards, and phone calls. But calls and letters were hardly the same as sharing kisses and seeing each other every day. In many ways, without Todd, Elizabeth was as lost and lonely as her brother. Although she and Todd had agreed to try to forge new lives for themselves, Elizabeth knew it was going to be hard.

"Mission accomplished," Jessica said smugly as she came back into the sunny, Spanish-tiled kitchen. "Steve said he would be right down." Just as Jessica was about to join the others at the table, the front door bell pealed. The family looked at one another with surprise. The Wakefields did not usually have visitors so early in the morning.

7

"Maybe it's a delivery for me," Mrs. Wakefield said. An interior designer, she sometimes received pieces she'd ordered for her clients at home.

The bell chimed again. "Well, I'm up. I guess I'll get it," Jessica said, dashing toward the door. A few moments later she returned with a sour expression on her face and Betsy Martin in tow.

"Betsy, what a nice surprise," Mr. Wakefield said cheerfully.

"Won't you join us for some breakfast?" Mrs. Wakefield asked, gesturing toward an empty chair.

"Sure, there's plenty," Elizabeth added, trying to make up for her sister's obvious lack of enthusiasm.

"Thanks, everyone, but I don't think I'll be staying that long. Steve called me about a half hour ago and asked me to meet him here."

Jessica caught her sister's gaze and looked away quickly. It was obvious that it wasn't her powers of persuasion that had gotten Steven out of bed.

"Here he is now," Betsy said, hearing his footsteps on the stairs.

Steven lumbered into the room. Dark circles under his eyes clearly showed how little sleep he had gotten the night before. " 'Morning, everybody," he said softly.

Worried by her son's appearance, Alice Wake-

8

field again asked Steven and Betsy if they wanted something to eat.

"Mom, I'm sorry. I'm just not hungry," Steven replied in a low voice.

Jessica went to the refrigerator, pulled out a pitcher of freshly squeezed orange juice, poured some into a glass, and handed it to Steven. "Here, at least have some juice. You look like you could use it."

Steven smiled ruefully. "I guess I can't turn down an offer like that."

"What about you, Betsy?" Elizabeth asked pointedly. She was growing furious with her sister. No matter how much Betsy had upset Steven the previous night, there was no reason to be intentionally rude to her.

"No, thanks," Betsy said, watching Steven finish his juice and place the empty glass on the table. "I think we're ready to go."

" 'Bye, everyone," Steven said, placing his hand lightly on Betsy's back and steering her toward the door. "See you later."

Elizabeth watched them disappear down the hall. "Well, what do you make of that?" she said a moment later.

"He certainly didn't seem angry with her," Mr. Wakefield commented.

Jessica sat back down at the table and gave her plate a look of disgust. "Thanks to Betsy Martin, my eggs are cold now."

Elizabeth glanced at her sister's plate. "Oh, you poor thing. There's not more than a forkful left."

Jessica drew herself up in her chair. "To think that my own sister, my identical twin, doesn't care if I have enough food to sustain me." She paused for effect and shook her shining blond hair. "Liz, you're so cruel."

"And you, Jessica, are such a wonderful actress," her twin said, smiling. "Your talents are wasted on us. I think it's time you were in another play."

"You two should team up," Ned Wakefield said, taking a sip of coffee. "Since Liz is our budding writer, she can write the parts, and, Jess, you can play them."

"Sounds good, Dad," Jessica agreed, "but I've decided the stage isn't big enough for me."

"Why?" Elizabeth giggled. "Are you planning on gaining a lot of weight?"

"Very funny," Jessica said, shooting her twin a withering look. "Actually, I've been thinking lately that I'm more suited to film. More money. More fame."

"Sounds terrific," Alice Wakefield put in. "Right now, though, the only roles we're casting for are the kitchen help." She got up and brought a few plates to the counter. "Anybody want to audition?"

"I don't mind trying out." Jessica grimaced. "But don't count on my taking it up as a career."

"Honey," her mother joked, "I never count on you for anything. Well, I've got some phone calls to make. Ned, what are your plans for the day?"

"I'm going to the office for a few hours. I need to bone up on the precedents for the case I'm defending." Mr. Wakefield had a flourishing law practice, which occasionally kept him busy on weekends and evenings. "So, girls, we leave the kitchen in your capable hands."

The twins sat quietly for a moment after their parents' departure, each girl lost in her own thoughts. Suddenly Jessica burst out with, "Gosh, Liz! The volleyball match is less than a week away. Maybe we should practice our serves this afternoon."

Jessica was referring to the charity volleyball match Sweet Valley High was playing against Big Mesa at the end of the week. The twins had volunteered to be on the team, along with a number of their friends.

"I don't know, Jess," Elizabeth replied. "I'd like to practice, but I'm going to be busy with Todd all day. Maybe tomorrow."

Jessica's reminder about the volleyball match brought a new worry to Elizabeth. She had no qualms about the game itself, although she had a feeling she needed to practice her serve. She was worried about the dance that was to follow the match. This would be the first big school event since Todd had left Sweet Valley. Dates weren't an absolute necessity, so Elizabeth wondered if she should make the effort to get one. On one hand there was no one special she felt like going with. On the other hand, she didn't want to go alone. She sighed. "Why do things have to be so complicated?" she muttered, barely realizing she'd said the words aloud.

Jessica looked at her sister. "Is something wrong, Liz?" she asked, her voice filled with concern. Despite their differences, the girls had a close and very special bond.

Elizabeth shook her head. "No, it's just something that'll have to be worked out with time."

Jessica knew better than to press her. Elizabeth would talk when she was ready. "OK, then. Which role did you want to try out for? Counter cleaner or dishwasher loader?"

Steven and Betsy walked quietly down the curved street past the well-maintained split-level houses that were similar to the Wakefields' home.

"How are things at school?" Betsy finally asked, breaking the silence.

Steven kicked a stone. "OK, I guess." He was a freshman at a college not far from Sweet Valley and lived in a dorm there. He used to come home only on weekends when he and Tricia were dating. After she died, he was so distraught that he had taken a short leave of absence from his classes. Lately he had been coming home more often, finding it a safe haven when things got rough. "Betsy," he said, "I'm glad you could see me this morning. I figured Jason would be teaching, so you'd be free."

Betsy smiled at the mention of her boyfriend's name. Jason Stone was a college friend of Steven's, and she'd be forever grateful to Steven for bringing the two of them together. Jason taught life-drawing classes every Saturday at the Sweet Valley Community Center. "Yes. Nothing interferes with Jason's teaching that class. He's a wonderful teacher."

"So I've heard."

They lapsed into silence and walked until they came to a small park filled with colorful flowers and unusual shrubs.

"Want to sit for a while?" Steven asked, indicating one of the old-fashioned stone benches.

"Sure," Betsy said, sitting down. Steven sat next to her. "It's so nice here," Betsy commented, looking around her. "I wish I could paint it."

"This was one of Tricia's favorite spots," Steven said, leaning over and plucking a blade of grass from the ground.

13

"Steve . . . maybe I came down too hard on you last night," Betsy said suddenly.

"No, you didn't, Betsy," he said, looking at her. "That's what I wanted to tell you. You were right. Cara Walker is a nice girl, but she'll never take Tricia's place."

"I was so worried, Steve," Betsy said, "I thought you were forgetting Tricia, and I couldn't let that happen." Betsy spoke with great intensity. "Tricia can live on, but only as long as we remember her."

"I know that," Steven answered. A look of understanding passed between them. Just then a bird landed in front of the bench and started chirping. Betsy looked at it and smiled brightly. "Did I ever tell you about the time Tricia was a robin in a school play?" she asked.

Steven smiled. "No. When was that?"

"When she was in the third grade. She was so cute." Betsy settled back and began talking animatedly. Steven listened quietly and let memories of Tricia ease his pain.

Two

Where is it? Jessica thought, as she kicked a pile of clothes across the floor. Her favorite bathing suit was missing. She looked through some things that were lying under her bed. *Nope, not there either.*

Elizabeth had once said that if you put a picture of Jessica's room next to one of a town devastated by an earthquake, it would be hard to tell which was which. The room's condition that day proved her point. But Jessica thought the messiness gave the room a comfortable feeling, and she liked it the way it was.

"Oh, well," Jessica said, sighing. "I guess I'll just have to wear Liz's pink one." Helping herself to whatever she found in her sister's closet was the way Jessica usually solved her clothing problems. Fortunately, Elizabeth was at the mall with her friend Enid, so she wouldn't be around to witness this particular theft.

Jessica pulled the belt of her terry-cloth robe tightly around her and padded toward her sister's room. As she was about to enter, she overheard her mother speaking on the hall telephone. The words Alice Wakefield was saying made Jessica stop dead in her tracks.

"A movie director! How exciting! How are you two related, Sharon?"

Sharon, Jessica thought. The only friend her mother had by that name was Sharon Egbert, Winston's mother. Could nerdy Winston, the clown of Sweet Valley High, be related to a Hollywood director? Jessica stood by Elizabeth's door, listening.

"Well, then it will be a reunion for you. I hope I'll get a chance to meet him," Mrs. Wakefield said.

So do I, thought Jessica.

"I can understand that," her mother responded after a pause. "If he's coming for rest and relaxation, he certainly wouldn't want people knowing who he is. I won't say a word. Oh, Sharon, one more thing about those lights you wanted . . ."

Jessica slipped into Elizabeth's room and went to the drawer where she knew she'd find her sis-

16

ter's neatly folded bathing suits. The hot-pink, strapless one-piece lay on top. Jessica pulled it out, and dropping her robe, put the suit on in one quick motion. Not bad, she thought, glancing at her perfect size-six figure in the mirror.

While Jessica finished getting ready to sunbathe, her mind was working at full speed. A movie director at the Egberts' was about the most exciting thing she could imagine! She couldn't wait to tell Lila and Cara. She was sure the three of them could learn his identity in no time at all.

Jessica strolled to the patio and set up a yellow-and-white deck chair. As she began rubbing tanning lotion on her slender legs, another thought came to her mind. Why should she tell Cara and Lila about this? They would only try to worm their way into a movie themselves. Stretching like a cat, Jessica settled herself into the chair. If anyone in Sweet Valley deserved a film career, it was she. *No partners*, Jessica concluded silently. *I'd better find out about this director myself*.

There was no question in Jessica's mind that she was going to meet him. It was merely a matter of how and when.

Deep in thought, Jessica closed her eyes. *Now let me see . . .*

*   *   *

"That's the best one so far, Liz," Enid Rollins said approvingly. "It really looks good on you."

Elizabeth looked over her shoulder so she could get a better back view of the spaghetti-strap dress in The Designer Shop's three-way mirror. "I'm not sure I'm crazy about the length, but you're right. It's better than anything else I've tried on in the last two hours."

Elizabeth started to change back into her blouse and jeans.

"Are you going to take it?" Enid asked.

"I guess so. I haven't bought a new dress for ages."

"You don't sound very enthusiastic about it."

"I'm not. If I hadn't agreed to be on the volleyball team, I'd probably pass on this whole affair." As Elizabeth spoke she ran a comb through her golden hair, then tied it back neatly with a navy ribbon. "It'll seem strange, being there without Todd."

"I know, Liz. It took a long time for me to get over George. Sometimes I still don't know how to manage without him."

Elizabeth felt a rush of sympathy for her friend. Enid and George Warren had been going together almost as long as she and Todd. Now George was dating Robin Wilson, and for a while Enid had felt as alone as Elizabeth.

After Elizabeth made her purchase, the girls strolled through the attractive mall.

"How about something to drink, Enid?" Elizabeth asked.

"Sure, let's go get a soda."

They wandered to the center of the mall and stopped at Howard's Delicatessen. A minute later, root beers in hand, Enid and Elizabeth seated themselves on a small wooden bench, where they had a good view of the Sunday shoppers.

"So your day with Todd was nice?" asked Enid.

Elizabeth smiled at the memory. "Terrific. I tagged along while he finished the business he came to town for, and then we had a terrific dinner together last night."

"Did you take him to the airport this morning?"

"No," Elizabeth said softly. "Neither of us wanted a public goodbye, so we decided Todd should go to the airport alone. It was easier that way."

"It sounds like you two got some things settled."

Elizabeth nodded. "We did. Although I still don't know if I'm going to try to find a date for the dance. What are you going to do, Enid?"

"I'm not sure. I suppose . . ." Enid looked up from her soda and was startled by the strange expression on her friend's face. "Liz, you look like you've seen a ghost."

19

Elizabeth stared back at her with troubled eyes. "Maybe I have. I could swear I just saw Todd coming out of that shoe store."

Enid whirled around to look. "Todd? He must be somewhere over Iowa by now."

Elizabeth grew more agitated. "Enid, it looked just like him."

"Do you think he missed his plane?" Enid asked.

"It's possible," Elizabeth said. "Maybe he went to my house, and they told him I was at the mall."

Enid's large green eyes grew wider. "Liz, you've got Todd on the brain."

"What are we sitting here for?" exclaimed Elizabeth, ignoring her friend's disbelief. "Let's go find him."

Elizabeth pulled Enid to her feet. "I'm sure I saw him heading toward the fountain," she said.

For the next half hour the girls searched the mall, darting in and out of shops, but they saw no one who even remotely resembled Todd. Finally Enid suggested that Elizabeth call home to see if Todd had stopped by.

"Nope," Elizabeth said, hanging up the phone. "Mom says she's been home all day and no one has even rung the door bell. "C'mon, let's go home," she said flatly.

Enid put her arm around her friend's shoulder as they walked down the parking lot toward the red Fiat Elizabeth and Jessica shared. "I'm sorry, Liz."

"No, I'm sorry. I led you on a wild goose chase," Elizabeth said, shaking her head. "I'm not even sure of what I saw now."

"Then you admit it wasn't Todd," Enid said sympathetically as she got into the car.

"It couldn't have been," Elizabeth answered, turning on the ignition. "Just call it a figment of my imagination, I guess. There's only one Todd Wilkins, and unfortunately, he's on his way to Vermont."

Three

Monday mornings always brought a flurry of activity to the Wakefield house, and this one was no exception. Mr. and Mrs. Wakefield had already dressed, eaten breakfast, and said their goodbyes. Jessica and Elizabeth were hurrying, trying to get ready for school. Steven, however, moved with uncharacteristic slowness. He seemed to be lost in his thoughts as he put his books and clothing into his duffel bag. Elizabeth had noticed Steven's mood, and when she passed Jessica in the hall, she gave her sister a worried look and nodded in Steven's direction. Jessica picked up the signal.

"So, Mr. University, ready to hit the books?" Jessica said, stopping at his bedroom door.

"Uh-huh," he grunted unenthusiastically.

"What time is your first class?" she asked, trying to start a conversation.

"Ten."

Still in her nightshirt and robe, Elizabeth crowded into the doorway. "You didn't use up all the hot water, did you, Jess?" she asked brightly.

"No, but I used all the shampoo," Jessica kidded. Steven didn't even smile. Instead he continued absently stuffing his gear into the duffel bag.

"Steve," Elizabeth asked after a pause, "is something wrong?"

Steven stopped packing long enough to answer, "No, I'm just in a hurry."

"You don't look like you're in a hurry," Jessica commented bluntly. "And by the way, where were you yesterday? You were gone practically all day."

"I was with Betsy," he answered, zipping the duffel bag closed and dropping it to the floor.

"Again?" wailed Jessica.

"Let's drop it, Jess," Elizabeth said, sensing a storm brewing. "We've got to get going."

"You're the one who isn't dressed," Jessica pointed out. She patted the collar of her oversized shirt and began to roll up her sleeves. "I'm ready."

"No you're not. That's my shirt, and I'd

24

planned to wear it today. So you'd better go change while I shower." Elizabeth spoke firmly and then walked off.

"Look, Jess," Steven said. "I don't want to talk anymore. I have to make a phone call before I leave."

Jessica was not about to be put off so easily. "Well, I hope you're calling Cara to apologize. You must have embarrassed her to death, running out on her at the party."

Steven flinched. He did feel guilty about that, but he was in no mood for a lecture from Jessica. "Cara wasn't my date. We talked for a while, that's all. It was no big deal."

Steven looked so sad and tired as he spoke that Jessica didn't have the heart to antagonize him. "I just hope Cara felt the same way," she said simply. "Have a good week, Steve."

As soon as Jessica left, Steven went down to the kitchen, picked up the phone, and dialed Betsy's number.

"Hello?" Betsy answered.

"Hi, Betsy."

"Steve, haven't you left yet?"

"I'm almost out the door. I just wanted to say goodbye and thank you."

"For what?" she asked.

"Oh, for digging out those old family photographs. And for that great drawing of Tricia you

25

did. I'm taking it back to school with me." He looked down at his duffel bag.

"Well, I knew you liked the portrait I did, but I wanted to do a smaller one that you could keep on your desk."

"I'm going to get a frame for it. It's terrific."

"I'm glad you like it," Betsy said sincerely. "Drawing it made me feel closer to Tricia again. So," she continued briskly, "are you coming home next weekend?"

"I guess so. Liz keeps trying to get me to buy tickets to some charity volleyball game and dance on Friday. Do you and Jason want to go?"

"Jason has to do something with his family. And I have a class that night."

"Then I think I'll pass on it too, but we will get together sometime next weekend, won't we?" Steven asked anxiously.

"Sure we will," Betsy agreed. "Call me when you get in."

Steven hung up the phone and picked up his duffel bag. He hoped he'd be able to spend time with Betsy the following weekend. She was his strongest link to Tricia. As long as he was with her, the memory of Tricia would never die.

The twins' red Fiat sped the few miles toward Sweet Valley High, a handsome columned building set on an expansive emerald-green lawn.

26

Elizabeth was doing her best to get to school on time, but her job was made harder by Jessica, who kept trying to shift the rearview mirror so that she could check her makeup. As Jessica reached out for the mirror one more time, Elizabeth swatted her hand playfully.

"I don't understand why you always get to drive," Jessica grumbled a moment later.

"You drove on Friday; it's my turn now. I'd think you'd like the chauffeur service. Besides, if you were driving how could you work on your face?" She glanced at her twin, who had now shifted the side-view mirror and was busy smoothing her eyebrows.

"Is Steve going to the dance this weekend?" Jessica asked, changing the subject.

"He hasn't decided yet. Say," Elizabeth inquired, "you've been pretty quiet about your own plans. Who are you going with?"

Jessica cleared her throat. "Actually, Liz, I'd rather not say."

Elizabeth gave her a puzzled look. "Why not?"

"Uh, he hasn't exactly asked me yet. But I can tell you it's a rather unusual choice."

Now Elizabeth was curious. Her popular twin had made several choices she hadn't liked at all. "It's not somebody wild, is it?"

"No," Jessica answered lightly. "This guy is just someone you wouldn't ordinarily think of me with."

27

"Oh," said Elizabeth, relieved. "Well, whoever he is, I'm sure you won't have much trouble getting him to invite you."

Of course I won't, thought Jessica. Winston Egbert had been crazy about her for ages. It was true that he hadn't paid her much attention lately, but Jessica was sure she could rekindle his interest in no time at all.

Jessica had decided the day before that meeting Winston's illustrious relative would be very simple. All she had to do was get chummy with Winston, go with him to the dance, and then invite herself to his house.

Once this Hollywood big shot saw her, the rest would be movie history.

"Why so quiet?" Elizabeth teased. "Thinking about your dream date?"

"Something like that," Jessica responded.

"If this guy's so special, how come you didn't get a new dress for the dance?"

Jessica shook her head. "I'm going to wear that sweater dress I bought at Foxy Mama's. It's not exactly perfect, but it will do."

"Well, if this mysterious date should come through, you can wear my new dress if you want to," Elizabeth said offhandedly.

Jessica sat up straight. "Really?"

"Nobody special is going to see me in it," Elizabeth said as she drove the Fiat into the student parking lot. "It may as well be put to good use."

Jessica considered her sister's offer. On one hand, it wouldn't really be fair to borrow Elizabeth's dress for a date with Winston. On the other hand, she didn't want to look shabby. Jessica decided a compromise was in order. "Thanks for the offer Liz. I'll tell you what—if I get the date, I'll wear the dress." She could already see herself looking fabulous in her sister's new dress.

The noise level in Room 103 was high when Jessica walked into her English class later that day. Groups of kids were standing around, waiting for Mr. Collins's class to begin. Some of them were talking about Lila Fowler's party, while others were speculating about the volleyball match later in the week. Jessica put her books down on her desk and went over to Guy Chesney and Emily Mayer, two members of Sweet Valley High's popular band, The Droids.

"Hi, you two," Jessica greeted them. "Gearing up for the dance?"

Guy pretended to play his keyboards. "Yeah. It'll be great to play at the Caravan. The acoustics are really good there. "What about you?" Guy asked. "How's your serving arm?"

"All ready." Jessica laughed, flexing her

biceps. Then she noticed how wan and tired Emily looked. "Hey, Emily," she said, "you look like you've been staying up late. Practicing hard?"

Emily gave a short, humorless laugh. "Hardly. How can I study or sleep when Karen is up all night, crying?"

"Is your stepmother upset about something?" Jessica asked, confused.

"Not that Karen," Guy put in. "Her new baby sister is named Karen, too."

"*Half*-sister," Emily said sullenly.

"Oh, that's right," Jessica said, remembering. "Your father and stepmother just had a baby."

"Yeah, so now instead of one Karen messing up my life, I've got two," Emily complained.

"Is it really that bad?" Jessica asked.

"Worse," Emily answered. "I thought once the baby was born it would at least get Karen off my back. But now she has even more to complain about. She says I don't help enough. I never offer to baby-sit. It seems I can't do anything right."

"Doesn't your dad stick up for you?" Jessica asked.

"Why should he?" Emily replied bitterly. "He's got a new wife and a new baby. He's all set."

"Take it easy," Guy said.

"Gee, it sounds awful," Jessica commiserated.

Then, out of the corner of her eye, she saw Winston laughing in the corner with a couple of kids. The bell rang shrilly, and Mr. Collins came striding into the room. A handsome man resembling Robert Redford, he was the target of many crushes among Sweet Valley High's female population.

"Good morning, scholars," he said with a grin as he took his seat behind the desk. "Before I start class, I want to get your choices for term projects. I hope you've all decided which American authors you'd like to study."

Jessica looked around in a panic. She hadn't given it a moment's thought.

"We'll go around the room," Mr. Collins continued. "If someone chooses your author, speak up. I'll assign you both to that subject, and you can work together."

Lila, who was sitting at the front of the class, turned and looked at Jessica. "Hemingway," she mouthed.

Highway? Jessica wondered what Lila meant by that.

Three students gave Mr. Collins their choices. Then it was Winston Egbert's turn.

"Are you going to do one of our American humorists?" Mr. Collins asked.

Winston sat up. "No, Mr. Collins. I'd like F. Scott Fitzgerald."

A moment later, Jessica raised her hand. "I wanted to do Fitzgerald, too," she said.

Surprised eyes from all over the classroom turned in her direction, though no one looked as shocked as Winston. Only Mr. Collins acted as if there was nothing strange about Winston Egbert and Jessica Wakefield working together.

When the bell sounded, Lila came up to Jessica as she was collecting her books. "Jessica, what's going on?" she asked. "What made you team up with the king of comedy?"

"I don't know," Jessica answered breezily. "I'm just interested in Fitzgerald, I guess."

"But I thought we would do Hemingway together." Lila pouted. "He's Mariel Hemingway's grandfather, you know."

"I don't think that's the kind of information Mr. Collins is looking for," Jessica said as the two of them headed toward the door.

"Uh, Jessica . . ."

Jessica whirled around. Winston Egbert was standing a few feet behind her. Lila stood at the door, waiting.

"I'll catch up with you in a minute, Lila," Jessica said. Then she gave Winston a big smile and moved toward him. "Yes, Winston?"

"Guess we'll be working together," he said, looking a little dazed. It wasn't so long ago that Winston would have given anything to share an assignment with Jessica. Since then he'd had several girlfriends, but that didn't mean he was immune to Jessica's charms. Still, Winston was also a little wary of her. He had seen her in action with too many other guys.

"Yes, and I think we should get started right away. Maybe I can come over to your house soon to talk about it," she said, looking up at him coyly.

"That would be great, but I'm not sure we'll be able to do it at my house. We're expecting guests, and things are kind of upside down over there. We might have to do it at your place."

Jessica tried not to show her disappointment. "Whatever," she responded casually.

"Well, see you later." Winston gave Jessica a small salute, turned, and almost tripping over his feet, left the classroom.

Darn, thought Jessica. *We didn't even have a chance to talk about the dance. We will, though. Winston Egbert, you don't know it, but this Friday, you're going to have the best time you've ever had.*

"How's that article on the charity game and dance coming, Liz?"

Elizabeth looked up from her copy to see Penny Ayala, editor of *The Oracle*, standing beside her. As usual, the student newspaper office was buzzing with activity during study hall, but Elizabeth had been so involved in her writing she had blocked everything else out, including Penny's arrival. "I'm almost finished," she said. "Want to read it?"

Penny peered over her shoulder. "Actually, I'm more interested in the length. The coach just called and said player rosters for both teams were in his office. Do you have room to put them in?"

Elizabeth scanned the page. "The players' names are pretty important." She smiled at Penny. "I'm sure I can fit them in."

"Good. Do you mind going to Coach Schultz's office and picking up the lists?"

Elizabeth pushed herself away from the desk. "I'm on my way."

Elizabeth was just down the hall from her destination when she stopped dead in her tracks. Todd Wilkins was coming out of Coach Schultz's office! "Todd!" Elizabeth called, shouting the name so loudly that several kids turned around to look at her. Elizabeth quickly moved toward the boy, but just then the bell rang, and students began streaming out of their classrooms. Elizabeth fought her way through them and got to the school's glass doors just in time to watch the boy climb into a shining blue convertible.

It wasn't Todd. Elizabeth could see that clearly now, but he had the same tall, athletic build and wavy, brown hair, cut in an identical style. He even carried himself in the same confident manner that Todd did. It was no wonder that Elizabeth had mistaken him for her boyfriend. Shaking a little, Elizabeth leaned against the door as she watched his car drive out of sight.

Who was he? she wondered. Was it possible that a boy who looked so much like Todd Wilkins had been going to Sweet Valley High and she didn't even know who he was? Her heart pounding, Elizabeth turned away from the door. She might not know who he was, but she was determined to find out.

Four

"Telephone, Jess," Mr. Wakefield called from the upstairs hall.

"Thanks, Dad. I'll take it in my bedroom." She turned to Elizabeth, who was helping her fix dinner. "Liz . . ."

"Go ahead," said Elizabeth. "I'll finish up. We were just about done anyway."

"Thanks," Jessica called over her shoulder as she dashed to her room. "Hello?" she said, picking up her brown princess phone a minute later.

"Hi, Jessica. It's Cara."

Jessica threw a few things off her bed and got comfortable. Her conversations with Cara were usually lengthy. "What's up?"

"I looked for you all day," Cara said. "I

37

haven't talked to you since Friday. Is Steve still upset about what happened at the party?"

Jessica kicked off her shoes. "He seems to be, Cara. Betsy Martin succeeded again in bringing on another case of the Tricia blues."

"That's what I was afraid of." Cara sighed.

"That was your golden opportunity," Jessica responded. "Couldn't you keep his mind off Tricia for one night?"

"We were having a good time," Cara said softly. "At least I thought we were. But then Betsy came along and started being abusive. The next thing I knew, Steve was running toward the door."

"I can't believe we let Betsy get her hooks into him. They spent the whole weekend together," Jessica informed Cara with disgust. "If you ask me, it's unhealthy."

"Don't be too hard on him," Cara said in a caring voice. "I know how it is when you miss somebody." Cara's parents had recently separated, and Mr. Walker had left Sweet Valley, taking Cara's younger brother with him. The experience had been difficult for Cara, and in many ways it had changed her. Although she had a reputation as a gossip and a flirt, Cara now displayed a sensitivity and maturity beyond her years.

"Look, I'm sorry about Tricia," Jessica said impatiently, "but Steve's got to start living again.

Hanging around with Betsy is only going to keep him tied to the past."

"I suppose you could be right," Cara admitted. "But Steve's got to do what he thinks is best."

"That's noble, Cara. But I say if you want him, you've got to go after him. Steve will be in next weekend, and if he doesn't phone you, you'd better call him."

The old Cara, the pushy Cara, would have jumped at this advice. But now she looked at the situation from Steven's point of view. "I don't know, Jessica. I think Steve should be around whoever makes him feel better."

Jessica rolled her eyes heavenward. "OK, but don't say I didn't warn you." Just then Jessica heard Elizabeth call from downstairs that dinner was ready.

"Cara, I've got to go eat. I'll talk to you later."

The moment Jessica hung up, the phone rang again. This time a deep, masculine voice answered her hello. It was Todd.

"So did you get back to chilly old Vermont all right?" Jessica asked. "I'm sorry I didn't get to see more of you while you were here."

"Well, it was kind of a rushed trip. Look, Jess, is Liz there?"

At that moment Elizabeth appeared at the door. "C'mon, Jess. We're waiting for you."

"Hold on, Todd. She's right here," Jessica

39

said, handing the phone to Elizabeth. "I'll tell Mom and Dad we'll start without you," she whispered as she closed the door behind her.

"Todd, hi!" Elizabeth said, sitting down on her sister's bed. "I didn't expect to hear from you so soon. Is everything all right?"

"Everything, except that I miss you," he answered huskily.

"Oh, Todd. I'm lonesome, too." She closed her eyes and pictured his warm smile, his coffee-colored eyes.

"So, what's going on? Anything special coming up?" he asked.

"Just the charity volleyball game and dance on Friday."

"If you want to go to the dance with some-body, it's all right with me. You know what we decided," Todd told her.

"We'll see," Elizabeth said. "What have you got on your social calendar?"

A little excitement crept into Todd's voice. "Actually, there is one fun thing. This girl, Gina—I don't think I told you about her—she's having a party next weekend at her family's cabin in the mountains, and she invited me today." Todd launched into a description of Gina and how exciting it would be to spend a week-end away with his new friends.

"Sounds good," Elizabeth said, though she

40

felt as if a cold hand were squeezing her heart. "What else is going on?"

Todd began to fill her in on some of the things he hadn't had a chance to talk about while he was in Sweet Valley. The longer he talked, the sadder Elizabeth became. Although one part of her wanted Todd to be happy in his new environment, another part was concerned that he was doing it with such ease. He seemed to have made a lot of friends already. Elizabeth barely said a word as Todd went on about people she didn't know and places she had never seen. Finally Todd wound down. "Liz, I'd like to talk to you longer, but this is going to cost me a bundle."

"I know," Elizabeth said, a lump in her throat. "I'll call you the next time."

"Great, but don't forget I'll be gone next weekend."

"No, I won't forget," Elizabeth said softly.

"It was great seeing you. I wish I knew when we'll be together again."

"Probably not for a long time," she answered, trying to keep her voice steady.

"Well, hang in there. I love you, Liz."

"I love you, too." Now tears were welling up in Elizabeth's eyes, and she knew she'd better get off the phone quickly. "Bye, Todd," she said. The moment she hung up, the dam holding back her tears burst. Elizabeth threw herself on

41

Jessica's bed and began sobbing. "It won't be long before he forgets all about me," she cried. Todd was starting a new life, and she was stuck in the same old rut. But, she thought, that wasn't the worst of it. She had honestly thought that her relationship with Todd would last forever. Now she wondered whether they'd be able to keep it going until the next time Todd visited Sweet Valley.

Five

Jessica stared across the cafeteria with distaste. There was Winston Egbert, juggling pieces of fruit from other people's lunch trays. *My date for the dance*, Jessica thought. *He ought to get a jester's hat and make up his face like a clown's.*

Lunch period was almost over, and students began to move toward the doors. Winston, losing his audience, put the apple and banana down and began getting his books together.

It's now or never, Jessica thought.

To Jessica's dismay, so far her campaign to get close to Winston had met with a surprising lack of success. Their paths had barely crossed in the last couple of days, and when they did, Winston was no more attentive to her than usual. They hadn't even been able to meet about their project. Either Jessica had cheerleading practice or Winston was busy. There was no time to waste now, so Jessica marched up to where Winston was taking a last gulp of milk and stood in front of him, blocking his way out.

"Hi, Win," she said, giving him a seductive look.

"Hey, Jess. What's up?" he asked, clearing his throat.

"Oh, nothing special. All ready for the charity dance tomorrow?"

"Yeah, sure," he said, glancing at the clock.

"What lucky girl are you taking?" she asked.

Winston looked surprised at Jessica's interest. "Me? I'm going alone."

Good, thought Jessica. At least Winston hadn't gotten a date. "That's a shame, Winston," she said aloud. "I'm sure there are plenty of girls who'd like to go with you."

"Oh, I'm sure there are, too," he answered, a grin on his face. "Got anyone in mind?"

Jessica pushed the hair out of her eyes with a languid motion. "Let me put it like this. What would you think about going to the dance with a terrific aqua-eyed blond?"

Winston turned unexpectedly serious. "Oh, you've been thinking about that, too," he said.

Jessica was a little surprised but answered

44

quickly, "Yes, I thought it would be a great idea."

"Me, too. That's why I asked Elizabeth to go with me last period," he said.

"You asked Elizabeth," Jessica repeated.

"Yeah, I thought she might feel lonely with Todd gone. But she told me she'd decided to go by herself."

Jessica brightened. "So you still don't have a date?"

"Well, actually, I only asked Liz to help her out. Like I said, I'm going alone. I'm in charge of refreshments, you know, and I want to give that the full Egbert treatment. I mean, I can't worry about the food and a date."

"Of course not," Jessica said. She couldn't think of a graceful way to get Winston to ask her out now, so she decided to play the compassionate twin role to the hilt. "Anyway, I'm glad you thought of asking Liz, Winston. I guess we both have her best interests at heart."

"She's a great girl. Uh, I've got to get to class, Jess. See you later." He loped across the cafeteria, leaving Jessica standing alone.

Up in the *Oracle* office, the staff was busy putting the final touches on the latest edition of the paper. Elizabeth, a pile of books in her arms, hurried across the room. She bumped into

45

Penny Ayala and knocked the photos Penny was holding to the floor.

"Oh, Penny, I'm so sorry," Elizabeth said as she slipped to her knees and began to pick up the pictures. "I hope I'm not this clumsy during the game tomorrow."

"Don't worry about it," Penny said, smiling.

Elizabeth straightened up and glanced through the photographs. "What are these?"

"Just some pictures that didn't make it into the issue," Penny answered.

Elizabeth was about to hand them back when the photo on top of the pile caught her eye. "Penny," she asked with excitement in her voice, "what's this one?"

Penny looked at the photograph in Elizabeth's hand. "That's Big Mesa's volleyball team for the benefit."

"Do you mind if I hold onto it for a while?" Elizabeth asked, her eyes sparkling.

"No," Penny told her. "I was just going to throw them out. But why do you want it, Liz?"

"There's someone on the team who looks familiar. Thanks, Penny." Elizabeth hurried to the window, leaving Penny shaking her head.

In the light Elizabeth looked at the picture closely. Sure enough, one of the players was the boy who looked like Todd. Her eyes scanned the list of names printed at the bottom of the photograph. There it was: Michael Sellers. Elizabeth's breath quickened. It was a crazy thought, but she wondered if Michael's personality was at all similar to Todd's. In any case, she wouldn't have to wait long to find out; Michael was sure to be at the game the following night. And Elizabeth couldn't wait!

When the twins arrived home later that afternoon, they were surprised to see Steven's Volkswagen parked in the driveway. Jessica and Elizabeth raced into the house, but no one seemed to be home.

"Do you think Steve's in his room?" Jessica wondered aloud. She peered up the stairs.

"Listen," Elizabeth whispered, holding up her hand. "There are voices coming from the den." As they moved toward the door, the voices became louder. Although they couldn't actually make out what was being said, it was clear that Steven and their father were in the middle of a serious conversation.

"Let's not stand here," Elizabeth said. "We'll find out soon enough what's going on."

Inside the den, Steven was slumped in his father's armchair, while Mr. Wakefield watched him with somber eyes from across the room.

"I never thought I'd be unwelcome in my own home," Steven muttered.

Mr. Wakefield began pacing the floor. "Steve, I didn't say anything of the kind. I just don't think you should be here when you've got another full day of classes left."

Steven looked up sadly. "I'm sorry. I just seem to have trouble staying in one place."

"Oh, Steve, you can't get rid of ghosts by running away from them," his father told him compassionately.

"You don't understand," Steven ran his fingers through his already tousled hair. "Tricia's not a ghost to me. She's real, and I want to keep her that way."

Mr. Wakefield chose his next words carefully. He stopped by the window and turned to face his son. "That's not possible, Steve. Tricia's gone, and in time that will be easier to bear. Until the day comes when you can remember her without guilt or longing—and believe me, that day will come—you must try to deal with the fact that Tricia's life is over and yours must go on."

"I'm not ready to let her go," Steven said stubbornly.

"Let me tell you a story." Mr. Wakefield sat down in a chair facing Steven. "When I was a junior in college, my best friend died in a car accident. I was devastated for weeks. I couldn't study, couldn't eat. Nothing seemed important."

Steven nodded. He understood very well what his father had gone through.

Mr. Wakefield continued. "Finally I realized that grieving wasn't helping my friend. He wouldn't have wanted that for me either. That was when I came out of my depression, but I never forgot him. When you were born I named you Steven, after him."

Steven sat in silence for a moment. "Dad." He cleared his throat. "I know you're trying to help. But no matter how deeply you cared about your friend, it couldn't be anywhere near what I felt for Tricia. I loved her completely," he burst out. "We were planning to spend the rest of our lives together. I'm not ready to forget about her, and I don't think I ever will be."

Mr. Wakefield shook his head. "OK, we'll leave it for now, but think about what I said, Steve. Please." As he left the room he paused to look back at his son. Head in hand, Steven was a portrait of despair.

When Mr. Wakefield walked into the living room where the twins were watching TV, they were full of questions.

"What's Steve doing here?" Jessica demanded.

"Is he all right?" Elizabeth chimed in.

"He's all right," Mr. Wakefield assured them. "He's just going through tough times. Listen girls, your mother's car is in the shop, and I have to pick her up. Hold down the fort, will you?"

After Mr. Wakefield left, the girls discussed their brother's situation.

"I don't think we should intrude," Elizabeth

49

commented. "He obviously wants to be left alone."

"I guess," Jessica answered uncertainly.

"He knows we're here for him, so I'm just not going to give him any advice unless he asks for it," Elizabeth said. "Do you want to watch this movie?" she asked, indicating the TV.

"No, I've seen it already. It's the general who poisons everybody."

Elizabeth shot her twin an angry glare.

"Oops, sorry," Jessica said, shrugging her shoulders. "I guess I'll go upstairs for a while."

As she walked toward the stairs, Jessica wondered what should be done about Steven. On one hand she thought her sister was right. Maybe Steven would be better off if they left him alone. But on the other hand, she thought the time was right to get tough with Steven. It had been months since Tricia Martin had died. It was obvious that he wasn't going to get better on his own. And with Betsy Martin hanging around, Steven didn't stand a chance to get back on his feet.

No, Jessica said to herself, *it's time my brother had a good talking to.*

She turned away from the stairs and walked back to the den.

"Come in," Steven's muffled voice called.

"Hi, big brother." Jessica walked to her

father's chair and sat down. "I want to talk to you."

Steven groaned. "You, too? I'm not in the mood, Jess."

"Look, Steve. I'm telling you you've got to get your mind off Tricia. And the way to do that is to start dating Cara."

"Here we go again."

"You were having a good time with her at Lila's party. She's nice, and you like her. You know you do— Steve, where are you going?"

Without a word, Steven had gotten up and had walked toward the door. "I'm going out to dinner with Betsy. Not that it's any of your business."

"Oh, great. So you can sit around and mourn Tricia. That sounds like fun."

"We'll do what we want," Steven said angrily.

"That's sick," Jessica muttered. "Steve, sometimes I think you don't even want to feel better."

This remark hit closer to home than Jessica knew, but Steven tried not to show it. He flung the door open to see Elizabeth standing there, a concerned expression on her face. Before she could say a word, Steven shouted, "And I don't want to hear anything from you either!" Roughly he pushed by her.

"Whew!" Elizabeth exclaimed, going into the room. "What was that all about?"

51

"I was just trying to give Steve a little sisterly advice."

"Jess, I thought we had decided—"

Jessica cut in. "*You* decided. I think Steve should be seeing less of Betsy and more of Cara." Jessica got up and brushed some lint from her skirt. "Cara would be good for him."

"Cara? She's a snob and a gossip. She's totally wrong for Steve."

"That's not very nice," Jessica pointed out.

"I'm sorry, but that's the way I feel. Steve's too smart to be taken in by someone like Cara."

Jessica's eyes narrowed. "That's all you know," she retorted. "Since her father moved away and they had to sell their house, Cara's changed. She never gossips anymore, and she's nice to everyone. Frankly, I think she's gotten a little boring."

"Oh, really? Well, I'm not so sure people change overnight." Elizabeth turned to leave. "And even if Cara has changed, it's up to Steve to find out for himself. I don't think he needs any more of your help!"

Six

Elizabeth popped her head into Jessica's room. "Almost ready?" she asked.

In her bright-red shorts and a red- and white-striped shirt, Jessica looked perfect for the volleyball court, but her sad expression contrasted sharply with her cheerful outfit. "Liz, are you sure I can't wear your new dress to the dance?"

"For the fourth time, Jess, the deal was you could wear it if you had a special date," Elizabeth explained. "But you're going alone."

"That's only because I wanted to keep you company," Jessica said.

"Right." Elizabeth smiled with amusement. She knew her twin too well to believe this excuse. "Sorry, Jess, as I told you, I've got a special reason of my own to look good tonight." *And his name is Michael Sellers*, she thought. "Finish laying out your clothes so we can dress quickly after the game."

Since the dance was being held at the Caravan, a local night spot, the twins had decided to leave their dresses at home, change there, and meet the rest of the gang at the Caravan.

"I guess I'm ready then," Jessica said, taking one more peek in the mirror. She saw her sister's reflection. "You look nice, too."

Elizabeth smiled. She was pleased with her appearance also. Her hair was pulled back in a french braid, which was flattering, yet practical for volleyball. Her navy shorts and blue- and white-checked shirt gave her a perky look. "Let's get this show on the road," she said cheerfully.

"Yeah, let's do it," Jessica agreed.

Before they left, the twins stopped to talk to Steven, who was sitting in the living room, watching TV.

"Steve, can't we persuade you to come with us?" Elizabeth asked one more time.

"No. There's a ball game on. I'm going to watch that," Steven answered without looking away from the screen.

"We'll be back after the match," Jessica reminded him, "if you change your mind."

"I won't. Have a good time, though." Steven

seemed anxious for them to leave, so the girls waved and went out through the kitchen.

Elizabeth drove quickly to Sweet Valley High. When they arrived, the football field across from the school was ablaze with lights. The volleyball match was to be played in the center of the field. The stands were already beginning to fill up with spectators.

"Hi, Captain," Elizabeth said, coming up to handsome Ken Matthews. Ken, who was leading the volleyball team, was also the captain of the Sweet Valley football team.

Jessica chimed in, "The Wakefield twins reporting for duty."

"Good," Ken answered in a businesslike manner. "It's time for our team meeting. Hey, Patman, Fowler, Pfeifer, get over here." Elizabeth watched as her teammates approached from different parts of the field.

John Pfeifer, sports editor of *The Oracle*, was usually too involved in writing about sports to play them. But he was a whiz at volleyball and was certain to be a valuable member of the team. Bruce Patman was an excellent tennis player and his wicked serve would translate usefully into his volleyball game. Lila Fowler's spacious home boasted its own volleyball court, and while she didn't like to get messy, Lila had a spring in her step that enabled her to jump high and spike the ball.

When the team was all together, Ken had them form a huddle, and he laid out the strategy for the game. All the while, Elizabeth kept glancing around and over the shoulders of her teammates, trying to get a peek at the Big Mesa team, which was just coming onto the field. In the space between Bruce Patman's and Ken Matthews's broad shoulders, she saw what she was searching for: Michael Sellers, looking toward the bleachers. Though her view was not very good, she could see him clearly for the first time. Like Todd, he was tall and slim but well built, and had a strong jaw and brown hair. He was laughing with a teammate, and his grin seemed so similar to Todd's that Elizabeth gasped. She looked around at her teammates to see if anyone had heard her. But everyone, including Jessica, was paying close attention to Ken's instructions.

"So everyone knows what we're going to do, right?" asked Ken. They all nodded, and though she hadn't heard a word, Elizabeth murmured her assent. Ken clapped his hands to break up the huddle. "Then let's go!"

Michael Sellers was captain of the Big Mesa team, and Ken went over to shake his hand. The Sweet Valley High band played the national anthem while the two teams stood at attention. At the song's conclusion, the crowd in the bleachers whistled and clapped, while Robin Wilson led the Sweet Valley cheerleaders in a school yell that was matched by a cheer from the Big Mesa squad.

As John and Jessica did a few warm-up exercises, the rest of the players took their positions. Coach Schultz was about to blow his whistle to signal the start of play when Sweet Valley High's principal, Mr. Cooper, nicknamed Chrome Dome because of his shiny bald head, took the microphone. "Young ladies and gentlemen," he began.

Jessica rolled her eyes at John. Chrome Dome Cooper was famous for his long-winded speeches, and it looked as if this one would be no exception. Sure enough, the principal launched into a number of subjects: the importance of charity, the necessity of good sportsmanship, the thrill of a well-played game. All were noble sentiments, and any other speaker would have inspired the players with them. But it looked as if Chrome Dome Cooper was about to put the crowd to sleep. Only the sight of Coach Schultz, standing with his whistle in his mouth and tapping his foot, finally made Mr. Cooper bring his oration to a close. At last Coach Schultz blew his whistle and started the game.

Since Bruce Patman had the strongest arm, he served first for Sweet Valley. He hit the ball with a bold overhand motion, sending it sailing over the net. Back and forth the ball flew, with a stocky girl from Big Mesa hitting it first, then

John Pfeifer making a swift return. Michael Sellers stepped in front of a teammate and hit the ball toward the back of the court in Elizabeth's direction. Brushing her bangs out of her eyes, Elizabeth tried to return Michael's volley but made the mistake of looking over at him for a split second before the ball came her way. In that hasty glance Michael looked so much like Todd that Elizabeth became flustered and missed the ball. It dropped to the ground, giving Big Mesa the serve. They scored a minute later after a short volley ending in a powerful spike past John Pfeifer. Fortunately Sweet Valley regained the serve when a Big Mesa player, a slender, athletic-looking girl, hit the ball straight to Lila Fowler, who spiked the ball over the net.

Sweet Valley was behind 1–0, and it was Elizabeth's turn to serve. As much as she wanted to concentrate on the game, she couldn't take her eyes off Michael Sellers; he looked so much like Todd. Hurriedly, Elizabeth served the ball overhand. But she used too much force, and it sailed beyond the Big Mesa baseline. The crowd groaned. For her next serve, Elizabeth attempted a safer underhand hit. This time she didn't use enough force, and the ball grazed the top of the net. Elizabeth lost the serve for Sweet Valley, and now a few jeers could be heard from the crowd.

"Liz, what's the matter with you?" Jessica whispered.

"Nothing. I'm just not warmed up yet," she replied.

Luckily, the ball was rarely hit to Elizabeth during the next few minutes of play. The score teetered back and forth and was tied a half hour later at fourteen points each, with Michael Sellers serving for Big Mesa.

Sensing that Elizabeth was the weak player on the Sweet Valley squad, Michael Sellers sent a powerful overhand serve in her direction. Elizabeth's timing was again thrown off, and she managed to reach the ball just as it was about to touch the ground. She scooped the ball up, but instead of going over the net, it went out of bounds. Big Mesa was now ahead by one point.

For the next play Michael Sellers attempted the same strategy and hit the ball straight to Elizabeth. This time John Pfeifer, who was standing behind her, ran up and returned the ball before she had a chance to hit it.

Although her teammates tried to cover for her during the rest of the game, the points Elizabeth had lost were valuable ones, and Big Mesa stayed ahead, winning the first game 15–13. During the break between games, Ken Matthews took Elizabeth aside.

"What's going on here, Liz?" he asked. "Whenever we played volleyball at the beach, you were one of the best players. Now it seems you can't hit the ball to save your life."

"I'm sorry," Elizabeth said, her eyes downcast. She wished with all her heart that she could concentrate on the game, but all she could see when she was on the court was Michael Sellers. "I'll try to do better in the next game."

Determined to keep her eyes off Michael, Elizabeth did improve in the second game, though she made one glaring error that cost her team the serve. Nevertheless, Sweet Valley won the game by four points, making a third game necessary to determine the winner of the match.

The band played a couple of rousing numbers while the teams took another break. Jessica took the opportunity to talk to Elizabeth, who was gulping some cool water.

"It's that guy who looks like Todd, isn't it?" Jessica asked knowingly.

Elizabeth felt her face grow red. "So you noticed him, too."

"Of course. He's gorgeous. Are you going to try and meet him later?" Jessica asked.

"I don't know." Elizabeth threw a troubled glance in Michael's direction. He was speaking to his coach. "He doesn't seem to notice me."

"Well, maybe if you played a little better, he would," Jessica said bluntly.

Elizabeth tried, but at the start of the third game, she was making as many mistakes as she had in the first. Sweet Valley was behind by five points when Ken called a time out.

"I've used up all my game plans," he admitted. "Does anybody else have any ideas?"

"We could try some soft spikes," Bruce suggested. "We haven't done much of that."

"OK," Ken agreed. "Anything else?"

Jessica said, "There's a move Elizabeth and I pull off, where I volley the ball to Elizabeth and she looks like she's going to hit it back to me, only she butts it over the net. We could try to fake them out with that."

No one said anything. Obviously they thought a strategy depending on Elizabeth's prowess wasn't likely to succeed.

Ken shrugged. "What the heck. We're losing anyway."

John clapped Elizabeth and Jessica on their shoulders. "Let's try it," he said, giving them a confident smile.

"Sure," said Elizabeth. She had forgotten about that old play she and Jessica used to use, but it was a good one. For the first time she had some of her confidence back. The team gave a few shouts and claps and ran back on the court.

Big Mesa had certainly been aware of the way Elizabeth was playing, so the first time the girls used their fakeout play, it worked beautifully. So beautifully that the Big Mesa team, thinking it was a fluke, was flabbergasted when the girls pulled it off two more times. Now they were only two points behind. Since Big Mesa was now on to them, they switched to a different strategy on the next play. Lila Fowler spiked the ball up and over the net just as it was hit to Sweet Valley. She jumped so high for a moment it seemed she was defying gravity. Sweet Valley was behind by only one point. The crowd started to go wild. Soon the score was tied. If Sweet Valley scored one point, they would win the game and the match.

Unfortunately, Lila grew tense under this extreme pressure. Both of her serves brushed the top of the net, and Sweet Valley lost the serve. The fans in the bleachers were now on their feet, knowing that at any moment the match would be decided.

Oh, no, thought Elizabeth. *It's Michael's turn to serve. I hope he doesn't hit it in my direction.* That was exactly what he did, however. The ball came straight toward her. Blocking out all the noise and Michael's face, Elizabeth hit the ball with all her might. Michael made a valiant effort to hit it back, but he missed.

Now it was Sweet Valley's turn to serve. Ken gave the ball a strong punch, but the ball was immediately volleyed back. Both teams played intently, keeping the ball in the air, back and forth, back and forth. Then it was sent Jessica's way. She tapped the ball lightly to Elizabeth, who was standing in front of her. Elizabeth gave the ball a short, hard spike right over the net. Big Mesa team members rushed at it from all directions; however, no one could get to it in time. The ball dropped, giving Sweet Valley the winning point. The players slapped hands and hugged. They had done it!

Students from both schools poured out of the stands to congratulate or console their respective teams. Some members of the Big Mesa team were shaking hands with their Sweet Valley counterparts. Elizabeth could see Michael chatting with Ken. She wondered if she should join them. *I'll just go over and say hi*, she told herself, but she couldn't quite get up the nerve.

"Hey, earth to Liz," Jessica nudged her. "We'd better get going."

"You're right," Elizabeth replied. "We don't want to be late for the dance."

"You certainly don't," a deep voice behind her said. "I'm leaving soon myself. What time can I expect you?"

Elizabeth whirled around and looked right into the coffee-brown eyes of Michael Sellers.

Seven

"Hello," Elizabeth said almost shyly.

"I don't know if I should be talking to you," Michael said, laughing. "But now that the match is over, I guess it's OK. Were you really playing badly in the beginning of the game? Or were you just pretending, to trick us?"

Elizabeth flushed. "Let's just say I improved as the match went on."

Jessica broke in impatiently. "I'm Jessica Wakefield, and this is my sister, Elizabeth."

Michael turned toward Jessica and gave her an appraising glance. "Oh, I know. I asked Ken Matthews about you. I'm Michael Sellers."

"Yes." Jessica smiled at him. "Big Mesa's captain."

Michael frowned for a moment, then gave Jessica a tight grin. "Well, unlucky in sports, lucky in love, or something like that. Actually, I'm usually pretty good at both."

"Is that so?" Jessica asked, giving Elizabeth a sidelong glance.

"Can I drive you two over to the Caravan?"

"Actually, we're going back to our house to change first," Elizabeth replied, looking up into the eyes that were so like Todd's. "But we'll be at the dance in about half an hour."

"Terrific, it'll take that long for me to get changed and get out there." He smiled at both girls, but his gaze lingered a second longer on Elizabeth. "Hurry back. I'm a stranger in town."

Elizabeth almost floated to the car. Michael Sellers had noticed her after all! Distracted, Elizabeth let Jessica drive the Fiat and didn't say a word during the entire ride.

When the girls got home, they noticed a strange car parked out front. Inside they heard male voices coming from the living room. The twins walked in to see Steven talking with his old friend Artie Western.

"Come on, Steve, let's go to the Caravan for a while. It'll be fun." Artie, a stocky boy with a friendly, open face, was a senior at Sweet Valley High. He and Steven had known each other since grade school.

"Oh, I don't know if I want to," Steven replied.

The twins looked at each other. Steven's uncertainty was progress from his earlier position.

Artie smiled when he saw Jessica and Elizabeth. "You think he should come, right?"

"We sure do," Jessica agreed. "It would be fun for the four of us to go together."

"We'd really like you to come, Steve. We're going to get dressed now, and we'll be down in ten minutes. Why don't you get ready, too?" Elizabeth urged.

After the girls went upstairs, Steven was silent. The game on TV had been boring; and with everyone gone, the house had been terribly lonely and quiet. Maybe he should go out for a couple of hours. Anything was better than staying at home, bored and alone.

"So, Steve," Artie pressed, "are you coming with us?"

Steven smiled. "I think I will."

The twins changed in record time. Elizabeth looked terrific in her new dress, and Jessica's sky-blue sweater-dress complemented her eyes.

A few minutes later the four of them piled into Artie's car and got to the Caravan just as the dance was going into high gear. The pounding beat of The Droids could be heard all the way to the parking lot, and the band sounded hot. They walked through the door and into the crowd. Jessica immediately excused herself and went to the far exit, where she saw Cara standing alone.

"I'm glad I found you in this crowd," Jessica said.

"Why? What's up?"

"Steve came to the dance." She nodded in his direction. "You should go over and say hi."

Cara shook her head. "I don't think so, Jess."

"Why not?" Jessica demanded.

"I haven't heard from him since Lila's party, and I just don't think he's interested."

"I'm not going to argue with you. Do what you want. But I don't see how you can get a relationship going while you're standing across the room from each other." Jessica started looking around for Winston.

"Jessica . . ." Cara said warningly.

"That's all. See you later." Jessica started across the dance floor without another word.

Despite her reservations, Cara began to consider Jessica's advice. Perhaps she should make the first move. Steven *was* going through a rough time; there was no question about that. And she could forgive him for his behavior at the party. After all, it wasn't his fault Betsy had created such a fuss. Now that Cara knew what it was like to lose someone that she loved, she sympathized with Steven. *I know what it's like to have people disappear from your life,* she thought. She missed her brother and father just as Steven missed Tricia. Perhaps they could cheer each other up, at least a little.

Cara decided to give it a shot. As she walked around the crowded dance floor toward Steven, she didn't notice Betsy Martin approaching him from the other direction. Betsy's art class had been canceled, and she had decided to see what was happening at the charity dance.

Steven tapped his foot to The Droids' newest song, "Crazy Love."

"This was a good idea, Artie," he said. As he turned toward his friend, he caught a glimpse of Cara walking in his direction. She looked lovely, and Steven couldn't stop his heart from rising when he saw her. Then he caught himself. Being with Cara the weekend before had caused him so much pain; he wanted no part of her tonight.

"Hi, Steve," Cara said uncertainly. "How's it going?"

Steven looked at her coldly. "OK, I guess." With slow deliberation he turned away to see Betsy Martin coming near. "Hi!" he exclaimed with relief. "What a surprise! I just got here myself—the twins talked me into coming. Betsy, I'm so glad you could make it."

Betsy smiled at Steven, then gave Cara a cool glance over his shoulder. "Me, too."

Without another look at Cara, Steven pulled Betsy aside. "I've got a lot to talk to you about.

Let's move over there, where we can have some privacy."

Cara stood frozen in humiliation. She was about to run off when she heard her name.

"Cara, would you like to dance?"

Cara looked up into Artie Western's friendly face. "C'mon," he said, taking her hand and leading her out onto the floor. "The Droids are playing a nice slow song."

While they were dancing, Cara was hardly aware of being in Artie's arms. Her attention was focused over his shoulder on the corner where Steven and Betsy stood talking. Once again Steven had shut her out of his life, she thought with anguish. But why? Steven's words echoed in her heart. What had she done to deserve this?

"You're a good dancer," Artie whispered softly into Cara's ear.

"Huh?" Cara blinked. "Oh, thanks."

They lapsed into silence for a moment, then Artie spoke again. "Cara, I've wanted to get to know you for a long time. Maybe we could go out tomorrow night and get to know each other better."

Cara was startled by Artie's invitation. Although Artie was a nice boy, and good-looking, Cara didn't think she should get involved with him. Quickly she racked her brain to think of an excuse, but none came to mind.

Finally, she forced herself to smile and said, "Well, sure."

"Great." There was no mistaking Artie's grin as genuine. He pulled her closer. "We'll do something special," he murmured.

Cara barely heard him. She was looking around for Steven and Betsy, but they were gone.

Across the floor Elizabeth was dancing with Michael Sellers. Michael had found Elizabeth soon after she arrived. Without a word he had confidently swept her out onto the dance floor, and now Elizabeth was reveling at being in his strong arms. Michael felt so much like Todd that dancing with him was almost like dancing with her former boyfriend. Elizabeth closed her eyes and leaned lightly against Michael's chest. It was strange to feel so comfortable with another boy. Elizabeth could barely believe it was possible. At that moment she was so mesmerized by Michael's resemblance to Todd that Elizabeth wondered if anything—even replacing the boy she loved—was impossible.

When the song ended, Michael abruptly pulled away from Elizabeth. "I'm starving," he told her. "Let's see what kind of food they've got here."

Elizabeth followed Michael to the refreshment table, which Winston had decorated and set with a lavish cold buffet. Michael, however, did not seem impressed. "Is this it?" he asked, grabbing a plate and filling it with sandwiches.

Elizabeth bristled a little. "A friend of mine is in charge of the food."

"Yeah? Well, maybe next time he should get some help," Michael said gruffly.

Elizabeth decided to ignore Michael's remark. Perhaps he was joking. But from the scowl on his face, she didn't think so.

They walked to a quiet corner, where a few chairs had been set up. "Have a seat, Miss Wakefield," he said with a flourish. "I want to get to know you better."

Elizabeth smiled and sat down. She still couldn't take her eyes off Michael.

"So," he said, taking a bite out of his sandwich, "you never told me why you were playing so badly at the beginning of the game."

Elizabeth flushed. "Don't you ever have an off night?"

"Rarely," he answered. "I just don't know how you guys did it. Luck, I guess." He took another bite of his sandwich. "Now, when it comes to football, I never have an off night."

For the next five minutes, Michael went on about how important he was to the Big Mesa football team, how likely he was to get a football scholarship from a big-name school, and how, when that happened, his father was going to buy him a sports car.

Elizabeth listened to Michael's monologue silently. Perhaps he was bragging because he was nervous. More than anything, she wanted to like Michael, but he was making it awfully hard. Elizabeth gave him a sidelong glance and noticed he looked less like Todd.

The Droids started playing again. Dan Scott, the bass guitarist, took center stage, while Emily Mayer started pounding out a beat on her drums. Michael put his empty plate under the chair. "Let's dance, Liz."

"Give me your plate," Elizabeth said irritably. "I'll throw it out."

Michael shrugged and handed her the plate, which she dropped in a nearby trash can. They started to dance, and Elizabeth felt relieved that the music was so loud she didn't have to talk to Michael. But the band soon switched to a slower song, and Elizabeth felt obligated to say something.

"Weren't you at Sweet Valley High last week?" she asked.

"Yeah, I was dropping off the player roster. Did you see me?"

Elizabeth nodded.

"You should have come up and said hello. It would have made my day."

That was a nice thing to say, Elizabeth told herself. *Maybe he's not so bad after all.* Once again

Elizabeth closed her eyes. It was easier now to pretend that Michael was Todd.

Elizabeth's dreamy mood was soon shattered by Michael's harsh voice in her ear. "What do you want, buddy?" She blinked her eyes open and saw Winston Egbert standing next to them.

"Sorry to interrupt," Winston said apologetically. "I wanted to ask Elizabeth for the next dance."

"Yeah, well, she's busy with me," Michael said gruffly.

"Michael!" Elizabeth exclaimed.

He looked down at her, a curious expression on his face. "What's with you?"

"You're being rude," Elizabeth declared.

"Listen, no jerk butts in on me," he told her forcefully.

"The only jerk around here, Michael Sellers, is *you*," Elizabeth said, disentangling herself from his arms. She turned to Winston. "I'm so glad you found me. Let's talk while we're dancing."

"Certainly." Winston smirked at Michael, who was staring at them openmouthed. "Better close your trap, *buddy*," Winston said, mocking Michael. "You're going to catch flies if you don't." With that parting shot, Winston and Elizabeth whirled away.

Anger flashed in Michael's eyes. Then he shrugged his shoulders and turned away.

"Who was that guy, Liz?" Winston asked.

"Just one of the Big Mesa volleyball players," Elizabeth answered as she watched Michael stride away.

"Oh, yeah. I guess I did see him on the court."

"Did you think he looked like Todd?" Elizabeth asked curiously.

"Todd? Oh, maybe a little. But he's such a jerk, he doesn't remind me of Todd at all."

Elizabeth nodded in agreement. "You're right," she said softly.

"Is something wrong, Liz?" Winston said with concern. "You seem kind of down."

"No, I'm fine." She smiled at him.

"Then let's dance!" Winston exclaimed. With that, he went into one of his crazy dance routines, which Elizabeth laughingly tried to follow.

When the song was over and Winston had gone back to the food table, Elizabeth walked to the sidelines, where Enid was standing.

"Elizabeth," her friend greeted her, surprise in her voice, "how come you're not with Michael?" Ever since Elizabeth had discovered the photo of Michael in the *Oracle* office, she had kept Enid abreast of the situation. Enid knew how much her friend was looking forward to meeting him.

Elizabeth sighed. "Oh, Enid. He turned out to be such a jerk. Rude, insensitive, obnoxious—he wasn't like Todd at all."

"Gee, I'm sorry, Liz," her friend said sympathetically. "That bad, huh?"

"Worse. How could I have been so dumb, thinking I could replace Todd?"

"Sometimes we just believe what we want to believe, Liz. Remember how I clung to George, even after he'd made it perfectly clear we were finished?"

"That was a hard time for you," Elizabeth remembered.

"Nobody held on to her fantasies longer than I did," Enid said.

Elizabeth leaned against the wall. "I guess it's hard to let go," she commented thoughtfully.

"It is. But, Liz, one good thing has come out of your experience with Michael."

Elizabeth couldn't imagine what she meant. "What's that?"

"You've learned that you can't rush things. And you can't expect to find another Todd."

"Nicholas, Michael," Elizabeth murmured. "I do keep trying to fill that hole in my life, don't I?"

"Yes, but you have to remember that not just anyone will do. You shouldn't rush things," Enid warned.

"I think I know that now," Elizabeth answered soberly.

"You just have to learn to take life as it

comes," Enid declared. She broke off with a laugh. "Listen to me, the voice of wisdom."

"You give good advice." Elizabeth threw her arms around her friend and gave her a hug. "And I thank you for it."

Enid hugged her back and smiled. "Hey, that's what best friends are for."

Across the dance floor Michael Sellers had found Jessica and was dancing with her. She was gazing up at him, pretending to be interested in his football stories. Actually, she was bored out of her mind with his egotistical monologue, and looking for an excuse to get away from him.

Just then Winston Egbert wandered by. That was the first time Jessica had seen him all evening.

"So then I made the most important play of the game," Michael informed her.

But before he could go on, Jessica interrupted him. "Michael, excuse me. I've got to talk to Winston."

"Winston," he said, clearly annoyed. "Who's Winston?"

"He is." She pointed in Winston's direction. Without further explanation Jessica dashed away from Michael, leaving him standing alone in the middle of the dance floor. He watched in disbelief as Jessica went up to the same boy who had caused all his problems with Elizabeth. "Jessica," he called out a moment after she had left, but she didn't even turn her head.

Michael Sellers was astonished. He simply couldn't figure it out. What was wrong with those Wakefield twins? And what did Winston have that he didn't?

Eight

The sun was streaming into Jessica's bedroom. At first she put her pillow over her head and tried to fall back to sleep. Then she remembered what day it was and bounded out of bed. That morning she was going to Winston's house to work on their English project. She wanted to look her best in case the Hollywood director had already arrived.

As she bathed and dressed, Jessica thought back over the previous night's conversation with Winston. He had been so distracted, worrying about his buffet table, that all she'd had to say was "Can I come over tomorrow so we can get started on our project?" and he had agreed.

With her hair brushed and flying loose, and

wearing a pair of jeans and her best sweater, Jessica felt ready to be discovered.

"My, don't you look terrific," Elizabeth said when Jessica pranced down the stairs and into the living room a few moments later.

"Thanks," Jessica said, settling herself into one of the beige armchairs across from the couch where Elizabeth was seated, leafing through a magazine. "Where is everyone, Liz?"

"Mom and Dad are out shopping, and Steve's washing his car."

Jessica looked out the window in the direction of the driveway. Steven was scrubbing his yellow Volkswagen so hard he looked as though he were trying to take the finish off it. "I wonder what kind of time he had last night."

"When we got home I saw him out on the patio with Betsy, reminiscing about Tricia." Elizabeth put her magazine down and became serious. "You know, Jess, I'm beginning to think you're right. Perhaps he *is* living too much in the past."

"And what about you?" Jessica asked. "Was being in Michael Sellers' arms like a trip back in time?"

Elizabeth could laugh about Michael now. "I think you know it didn't work out quite like that. I'm sure he said something to you."

Jessica crossed her legs and got comfortable.

"Yeah. He stopped talking about himself long enough to tell me how rude you were."

Elizabeth snorted. "Me, rude? That's a good one."

"What did you do to the guy anyway?"

"I dumped him for Winston," Elizabeth told her with a sly grin.

Jessica's eyes grew large. "Oh, he really must have gone crazy when I did the same thing."

"He did. Enid and I were watching."

The girls giggled. "He deserved it, though," Jessica continued. "Boy, I've never met someone who was so impressed with himself."

Elizabeth sobered. "Nothing like Todd."

"Better luck next time," Jessica said lightly. "Only next time better not come quite so quickly."

"Funny, Enid said almost the same thing."

"Then for once I agree with her." Jessica stuck out her hand and gave Elizabeth's a little shake. "Elizabeth Wakefield, welcome to the land of the living."

"Thanks. I wish we could say the same thing to Steve," Elizabeth said.

"Hey, are you using the car today?" Jessica asked.

"No, I'm playing tennis with John Pfeifer, but he's going to pick me up," Elizabeth said.

"John Pfeifer? Love blooms on the volleyball court," Jessica teased.

"You know we're friends from *The Oracle*. There's nothing going on between us, except that we both like tennis."

"OK, I believe you. So where are your car keys?"

Elizabeth gave her sister a weary look. "Where are yours? Oh, never mind." She went to the small table in the entrance hall, where her purse was sitting, took out the keys, and tossed them to Jessica, who caught them deftly. "What do you need the car for anyway?"

"I'm going over to Winston's. To work on our English report," she added quickly.

Elizabeth gave her an appraising look. "You're pretty dressed up for Winston Egbert. What's going on between you two, anyway?"

"I'm not dressed up for Winston," Jessica said mysteriously. "And I can't help it if we were assigned to the same English paper." She rose and grabbed her purse from the coffee table. "Have fun with John," Jessica told her sister as she beat a hasty exit. She wanted to leave before the questioning became intense.

Steven stopped soaping his car long enough to wave to Jessica as she backed out of the driveway. Sometimes he wished he could be more like his carefree younger sister.

That morning Steven was feeling bad about all kinds of things. First, there was Cara. Her hurt, humiliated expression on the dance floor had stayed with him, and it was awful knowing he had been the cause of it. Then there was the matter of his true feelings about Cara. He knew it was time to be honest with himself. He was attracted to Cara. There was no doubt about it. He had known for sure when Artie had called him that morning to say he had made a date with Cara for that night. Steven had felt a sharp stab of jealousy.

Then there was Betsy. He wondered whether his family was right about Tricia's sister. Was she trying to hold him too tightly to the past? He pushed the disloyal thought aside. No, his conversations with Betsy enabled him to remain true to Tricia.

Tricia. Just her name conjured up images in his mind. None of this would be happening if Tricia were still with him! Steven threw the sponge back into the soapy water and sat down on the front lawn. He missed her. Putting his head in his hands, Steven began to sob.

Elizabeth, who had been watching her brother from the living-room window, saw him crying. She walked out the front door and went over to him. "Oh, Steve," she whispered as she sat down.

He looked at her with red-rimmed eyes. "I'm so mixed up, Liz," he said, taking short breaths.

"I know." She patted his knee. "But it'll get better, Steve."

"Will it?" he asked, his face etched with suffering. "Sometimes I wonder."

Elizabeth sighed deeply. Sometimes she, too, wondered when Steven would at last get over the pain of losing Tricia Martin.

Jessica walked up the steps of the Egberts' Spanish-roofed house and rang the doorbell. A few moments later, she heard footsteps and the door swung open.

"Jessica," Mrs. Egbert greeted her, "come in. Winston told me he was expecting you. He's around here someplace."

Like her son, Sharon Egbert was tall and thin. But instead of appearing gangly, as Winston did, Mrs. Egbert had a look of sophistication. Jessica's heart dropped, however, when she saw how Mrs. Egbert was dressed. Surely she wouldn't be wearing beat-up jeans and a stained sweat shirt if she had important guests visiting. There were even a dust cloth and wood polish on the hall table.

"Forgive my appearance," Mrs. Egbert said, as she led Jessica into the entrance hall. "I'm just getting the house ready for my cousin Marty's visit."

"That's very nice," Jessica said, deciding to see how much information she could get from Mrs. Egbert. "Does he come to visit often?"

"No, I haven't seen Marty in ages. Sit down, Jessica. I'll see where Winston is."

Jessica didn't want Mrs. Egbert to leave. She wanted to find out more about Marty. "Were you and your cousin close as children?" Jessica asked quickly.

"Why, yes." Mrs. Egbert turned back toward Jessica. "I was practically raised with Marty's family, so it will be terrific to get together again."

"It's a shame he can't get here more often," Jessica commented pointedly.

"His work keeps him traveling," Mrs. Egbert said.

"What kind of business is he in?" Would she tell her, Jessica wondered.

"Oh, he has a very important position—" Mrs. Egbert began. Just then Winston entered the living room.

"Hi, Jess," Winston said warmly. "Ready to get started?"

"Sure," Jessica replied, barely giving him a glance. "When is your cousin arriving, Mrs. Egbert?"

"In a few days. Well, I'll get out of your way." Mrs. Egbert smiled at Jessica. "I guess we'll be seeing quite a bit of you, Jessica."

"Oh, yes. Winston and I have a ton of work to do on this project."

"You're welcome here anytime, dear. It's nice to see you."

Jessica gave her a winning smile. "Thank you, Mrs. Egbert." When Mrs. Egbert left the room, Jessica turned toward Winston. "How long do we have to work today?"

"I think we need to work all afternoon," he told her.

"Then let's get at it." Jessica sighed. Spending the whole day with Winston Egbert was not her idea of fun. *But maybe*, she thought, *this is what they mean by the high price of fame.*

Nine

"Do you think Cara would like to go to a movie tonight, Steve?" Artie asked Steven on the phone.

Steven nervously rubbed the phone receiver. "I guess so, Artie," he said, trying to be patient. "That sounds like a good idea." Artie was such a nice guy and a good friend. Steven didn't want to be rude to him. But he didn't feel like helping to plan Artie's date with Cara either. He had already been on the phone for a half hour. Steven was relieved when he heard the door bell ring downstairs.

"Look, Artie, our pizza is here, so I've got to go. Have a good time tonight, OK?" A moment later he had hung up the phone.

Since Mr. and Mrs. Wakefield had gone out to a dinner party, Steven had suggested to the twins that they order a pizza from Guido's. By the time Steven got downstairs, Jessica and Elizabeth were already seated around the kitchen table, each with a slice of pizza in hand. The open cardboard box on the table emitted a delicious, mouth-watering aroma. Jessica had already taken a bite of the pepperoni slice she was holding, and Elizabeth was about to start eating a piece that came from the sausage side of the pizza.

"Gee, you didn't have to wait on my account," Steven joked. He pulled up a chair and peeked into the box. "Hey, what do you know, there's still some left."

"Funny, Steve." Jessica wiped a spot of tomato sauce off her chin. "Mom and Dad are always bugging me about talking on the phone too much, but I'm nothing compared with you."

"Who were you talking to for so long?" Elizabeth asked.

"Artie," Steven answered. He didn't feel like getting into a discussion of Artie and Cara's date, but he had a feeling that Jessica would not want to drop the subject.

"Cara doesn't really want to go out with him, you know," Jessica informed her brother.

"Why not?" Steven asked, trying not to show much interest. "Artie's a nice guy."

"Sure he is," Jessica agreed. "He's just not Cara's type."

Elizabeth put down her slice of pizza to join the discussion. "And I suppose Steve is."

Jessica didn't like the tone in her sister's voice. "I'd like to know what's wrong with Steve and Cara seeing a little more of each other?"

"I just don't think they're right for each other," Elizabeth insisted. She gave a nervous, sidelong glance in Steven's direction.

Jessica abruptly put her glass down on the table. "Everybody thinks you're so kind and generous, Liz." She reached for another slice of pizza. "But you refuse to give Cara the benefit of the doubt."

"I'm sorry. Cara has pulled too many nasty stunts and told too many secrets for me to think she'd be a match for Steve."

"You were ready to forgive Betsy Martin anything," Jessica retorted angrily, "but just because Cara's made a few little mistakes, she's not good enough for you."

"Can't you ever stop playing matchmaker, Jess?" Elizabeth said.

"OK, that's it!" Steven thundered, his hand slapping the table. "Stop talking about me as though I'm not even here."

Both girls looked up, startled. In fact, they had both gotten so engrossed in their conversation, they *had* forgotten their brother was in the room.

Steven continued furiously, "I can't believe you two. Jessica, you keep insisting that I go out with Cara without ever asking me what I want to do. And, Liz, Jessica is right. How can you be so insensitive? Cara has made mistakes, but so have we all. There's no excuse for your misguided ideas about Cara!"

After Steven's outburst, Elizabeth sat perfectly still, her face red with embarrassment. But Jessica wasn't about to be quiet, no matter how forceful her brother's tone. Besides, in light of Steven's recent behavior, Jessica thought a good argument might be just the thing to get him back on track.

"That was a nice thing to say, Steve," she said forcefully. "I mean, it's nice of you to defend Cara here in the house. What I'd like to know is, why are you afraid to go out and be seen with her?"

"*Afraid?*" Steven sputtered. "Why should I be afraid?"

Jessica swallowed a bit of pizza. "I don't know. Maybe you're afraid of what people will think about your dating someone new. Or maybe you're afraid of what Betsy will say if you start seeing Cara."

Steven got up, his fists clenched in anger. He pushed his chair out of the way and walked to the sink, his back toward the twins. "That's crazy."

"Is it?" Jessica replied. "I think you're terrified of what Betsy will say if you start seeing someone new."

"Jessica!" Elizabeth exclaimed, shocked.

Steven turned and faced Jessica, his brown eyes blazing. "I don't care what Betsy says," he spat out. "I can do whatever I want!"

"Then why do you keep avoiding Cara now, after you've had some good times together? No, you do more than avoid her. You're incredibly rude."

Steven slammed his fist on the counter. "I've told you, Jess, stay out of it. I'll live my life the way I want."

"OK," Jessica said. She shrugged. "But remember Cara's got one advantage over Tricia. She's alive."

Steven stood stunned for an instant, as though Jessica had slapped him. Then, without a word he turned and rushed out of the room.

Elizabeth glared at her sister. "How could you, Jessica Wakefield?" she asked, her voice shaking. "That was the cruelest thing you've ever said."

Now Jessica let her true emotions show. Her voice quivered, and her eyes filled with tears. "I'm sorry, Liz, but sometimes you have to be cruel to be kind. We've tried over and over to give Steve our love and sympathy, but he just keeps falling deeper into his depression over

91

Tricia. I thought maybe shocking him might do the trick.''

Elizabeth looked through the glass doors leading outside. She could see Steven on the patio, his head in his hands. "I don't know, Jessica. You may have hurt him so badly that he won't get over it for a long, long time." Elizabeth grabbed her plate of pizza and stalked out of the room.

Although it was unusually warm that evening, even for California, Steven shivered a little as he sat outside. He tried to push aside the things Jessica had said to him, but they kept surfacing, demanding attention.

Though he didn't want to admit it, he knew Jessica was right about both Elizabeth and Betsy. It bothered him that Elizabeth wouldn't give Cara a chance. He valued his sister's opinion, and he couldn't imagine dating a girl she disliked. He knew Cara had changed, and if Elizabeth just got to know her, she would like her. From his own experience Steven knew Cara was a warm and sensitive person.

The more serious problem was Betsy Martin. After Tricia's death, Betsy had stayed with the Wakefields, and in that time she and Steven had become very close. Being with Betsy and talking about Tricia was a safe, if bittersweet, way to spend his time. Steven knew fate had charged him and Betsy with the responsibility of keeping Tricia's memory alive. And that brought Steven to the one fear that Jessica hadn't mentioned, the deepest fear of all. Steven was afraid he would forget Tricia, and so lose her forever.

He admitted to himself, for the first time, that it was getting harder and harder to picture Tricia's face. It was even more difficult to hear the sound of her laughter. He had tried to hold firmly onto her memory, but with each passing day, she became more difficult to cling to. Keeping Tricia with him was like trying to hold a handful of sand.

Steven stayed on the patio for a long time, thinking things through. Finally, with his bones aching from his cramped position on the chair, he pulled himself up and went into the house.

He had come to a decision while he was outside. He would call Cara and apologize to her. He owed her that, at least. He glanced at the clock in the kitchen. No doubt Cara was out with Artie, but he could call and leave a message. Even that first step would ease his guilty conscience a little. Grabbing the local directory, he looked up Cara's number and scribbled it on a piece of paper, then quickly, as though not to lose his nerve, he began to dial. To his surprise, Cara answered the phone.

"Cara, is that you?" Steven asked.

"Yes, who's this?" she asked.

"It's Steve."

There was a moment's pause. "Steven, I didn't expect to hear from you."

"Actually, I didn't think I'd be able to get you tonight," he responded. "I thought you'd be out with Artie."

"No, I decided to ask for a raincheck," Cara said softly. "It didn't seem fair to go out with him when I knew I wouldn't be very good company."

"Oh," Steven said, momentarily at a loss for words. Then he remembered the reason for his call. "Cara, I want to apologize to you. I mean, for running off like that at Lila's and the way I acted at the dance last night."

"It's all right, Steve. I know things have been rough for you lately."

"Well, I shouldn't have taken it out on you."

There was an awkward pause, then Cara said, "OK, I appreciate your calling." She sounded as if she was about to hang up. Suddenly Steven realized that that was not at all what he wanted her to do.

"Cara, I'd like to see you tomorrow," he blurted out.

"See me?" Cara seemed taken aback.

Steven took the plunge. "Yes, uh, maybe we could do something together."

Cara sensed the hesitation in Steven's voice. She didn't want to push him into anything, though her heart swelled with happiness at the idea of their having a real date. A thought struck her. Maybe it would be too difficult for him to be alone with her. Perhaps he would prefer to be around a group of people.

"Bruce Patman is having a splash party tomorrow afternoon," she suggested. "Would you want to do something like that?"

The last thing Steven wanted to do was attend a party. But he understood why Cara asked. "Actually, Cara, I'd rather just spend some time alone with you. How does a picnic sound?"

"A picnic would be great," Cara replied gently.

"Why don't I come over tomorrow afternoon around one, if that's OK?" Steven was anxious to make the arrangements before he changed his mind. He was already feeling pangs of guilt for making a date with Cara. What would Betsy say if she knew?

"One will be fine," Cara said. "I'll put together some food, and we'll decide where to go tomorrow. And, Steven, I'm looking forward to it," she added.

"Bye, Cara." Steven's hand shook as he hung up the phone. *Now I've done it*, he thought to himself.

Steven showed up at Cara's apartment the

next day promptly at one. He had told his family he'd be gone for most of the afternoon but hadn't been specific about his plans. Elizabeth probably would have been critical if she had known he was seeing Cara, while Jessica would have been ecstatic. He wasn't in the mood for either reaction. Besides, he wasn't sure how this meeting with Cara would end up, and it would be easier if no one knew it was taking place.

"Hi, Steve," Cara said as she led him into the apartment. She and her mother had recently moved there. It was pretty and modern, but it never quite felt like home to Cara.

Cara was wearing a simple white sun dress that complemented her long dark hair and olive complexion. Just looking at her, Steven felt some of his anxiety draining away.

"Cara, you look terrific," he said, giving her an admiring glance.

"Thanks," she said. She offered him a seat in the living room. "Have you had a chance to think about where to go?"

"Actually, I did come up with one. How do you feel about having our picnic at the zoo?"

Cara's face brightened. "I love the zoo. That's terrific."

Steven gave her a warm smile. "I just had a feeling you'd like to see some monkeys besides me."

"They're my favorites," she agreed.

96

"Then let's go!" Steven said, rising.

The sun shone brightly as Steven and Cara took the short drive up the coast to the regional zoo. Once there, Steven felt the mantle of sadness fall away from him for the first time in ages. He and Cara wandered throughout the zoo, watching the leathery elephants spray each other with their trunks, the proud lions roaring at visitors, and the chattering monkeys swinging from vine to vine. Finally, they settled down in the little park area with the picnic basket Cara had packed. Steven spread the old, gray army blanket he kept in his car and bought some drinks from the refreshment stand. While he was gone, Cara took out the checked napkins from the wicker basket and laid out fried chicken, pasta salad, and a chocolate cake.

"I'm impressed," Steven said as he stretched his tall frame out on the blanket. "I didn't know you were such a good cook."

"I'm not," Cara confessed. "I bought the chicken and the salad."

"Hey," Steven said, sitting up. "That's cheating."

"But I baked the cake," Cara declared, "with my own two hands." She held them out for Steven's inspection.

"And lovely hands they are, too." Without thinking, Steven took one and put it to his lips. As soon as he felt the touch of her skin, however,

97

he dropped her hand as though it were on fire. "I'm sorry," he told her, eyes downcast.

Cara gave him a steady look. "I don't think it's me you're apologizing to."

Steven met her gaze. "Maybe not. All I know, Cara, is that today I feel more relaxed than I have in a very long time. Let's try to concentrate on that, shall we?"

Cara beamed. "That's fine with me." She deftly changed the subject. "Now, here. I fixed you a plate of chicken and pasta salad, and even if I didn't make it, it's very good."

"OK, you talked me into it. I'll eat it."

"As if there were any doubt." She laughed.

"No, I guess you're right." He grinned. "But let's not spend too much time here. We've still got a date with two gorillas and a few seals."

Ten

Jessica and Elizabeth were sitting on the outdoor patio at Sweet Valley High, having lunch and watching the other students around them. On balmy blue-skied days like this, they sometimes went outside and worked on their tans instead of sitting in the cafeteria.

"So, did you talk to Cara?" Elizabeth asked, twisting the strands of her side-swept ponytail.

"Oh, I talked to her," Jessica responded, searching her purse for her sunglasses, "but she didn't tell me much."

"Did she actually say she was out with Steve on Sunday?"

"Yes. She said Steve wouldn't mind if she told me that much. I wonder how he knew I would

99

ask? Anyway, she didn't say a word after that. I swear, Cara's a completely different girl now."

"Well, I'm glad of that," Elizabeth said. "Still, I wouldn't mind hearing a few more details."

"Well, all she said was that she spent Sunday with Steve, and if I wanted to know more about it, I would have to ask him. I told her I already had." Jessica remembered how she and Elizabeth had teased their brother Monday morning before Steven went back to school, asking him where he had been the day before and why he was in such a happy mood. Steven had smiled benignly, but hadn't offered any clues.

Elizabeth gave her sister an approving glance. "I've got to hand it to you, Jess. I thought coming down so hard on Steve was a terrible idea, but now it looks like it was the right thing to do."

Jessica gloated. "It's about time I got some credit," she said. "If I didn't have other career plans, I'd consider becoming a psychologist."

"Thank goodness you're doing something else. I can just see you driving all your patients crazy."

"Very funny, sister dear."

Elizabeth looked at Jessica curiously. "By the way, what other career plans do you have in mind? Your mysterious comings and goings wouldn't have anything to do with that?"

"Uh, sort of," Jessica answered vaguely. For a second she considered changing the subject. But she was bursting to tell someone about her plans, and she didn't know a better listener than Elizabeth.

"Liz, remember when we were talking about my being in the movies?" Jessica took off her sunglasses and looked into her sister's eyes.

Elizabeth smirked. "Sure I do, Jess. Oh, no, did I forget to tell you? Harrison Ford called last night. He wants you to be in his next film."

"Ha-ha, very funny. It just so happens that I'm about to be discovered," Jessica informed her.

"Oh, really?" Elizabeth replied. "And how, may I ask, is this going to happen?"

"Liz, it's so exciting! By the end of the week—" Jessica looked up to see Winston Egbert walking across the crowded campus. She jumped to her feet. "Winston! Hey, Winston, wait up!" she shouted. "I'll tell you the rest of this later, Liz. I've got to talk to Winston."

Elizabeth couldn't understand Jessica's eagerness to be with Winston lately. In the past, she'd pretty much ignored him. Could she actually be attracted to him? Elizabeth wondered. It was going to be hard enough to accept a pairing of Cara and Steven, if that should come about. But a Winston-Jessica relationship? That was out of the question! Elizabeth looked at her watch. The period was almost over. She got up, straightened her clothes, and picked up her books. As she ambled through the cafeteria, she saw Cara Walker just ahead. Elizabeth decided to go up to her and hurried a little to fall in step beside her.

"Hi, Cara," she said tentatively when they were out in the hallway.

"Hi, Liz," Cara responded, looking a little surprised.

"Can we talk for a moment?"

Cara hedged. "I've got to get to the library."

"That's all right. I'll walk partway with you, OK?"

"Sure." Cara hoped Elizabeth wouldn't want to talk about her day out with Steven. He had asked that she not discuss the details of their date with anyone. And while he said he was going to tell his sisters they had gone out, he didn't want anyone else to know. Cara respected Steve's wishes on the matter. She hoped Elizabeth wouldn't press her with questions she shouldn't answer.

"Cara," Elizabeth began, "I know Steve asked you not to discuss your date, and I respect that."

"I'm sorry, Liz," Cara told her sincerely.

"That's all right. Actually I just want to apologize to you."

"For what?" Cara asked, surprised.

"I told Steve I didn't think you were right for each other, Cara. That was wrong of me. I saw Steve after your date. He was like a different person. If you can make my brother that happy, I

102

want you to know that I was mistaken." By now they had reached Elizabeth's classroom. "This is as far as I go," Elizabeth said.

"Liz, I don't know what will happen with me and Steve, but I appreciate your telling me this. Thank you. I really mean that."

"No, Cara, thank you—for making Steven happy, I mean."

A blush crept up Cara's cheeks. She smiled shyly.

Elizabeth returned the smile. "And, Cara," she said, "I hope we can be friends."

Cara nodded. "I hope so, too, Liz." With that, she nodded and rushed off in the direction of the library.

"Hurry up, Winston," Jessica implored. She and Winston were in the student parking lot, trying to get his old, broken-down Volkswagen started. Too many people had already begun to notice how much time she was spending with Winston. Being stuck with him in the parking lot was the last thing she wanted.

"Maybe I auto have this car fixed," Winston joked.

"What you 'auto' do," Jessica said archly, "is dump this thing in the nearest junkyard."

"Shh," he said, trying the ignition once more. "You're going to hurt her feelings."

Jessica's blood pressure was rising, but she whispered to herself: *Keep calm. Think fame, sable coats, Academy Awards.*

The ignition finally turned over. "There," Winston said. "That wasn't so bad. Was it?"

Jessica gritted her teeth. "Not bad at all."

"So," she asked conversationally once they were under way, "have your guests arrived yet?"

Winston honked the horn as Ken Matthews drove by, and Jessica thought she would die of embarrassment. "Yup," Winston replied. "Marty and his wife got in last night."

Jessica turned toward him, excitement spilling over. "I'd like to meet him."

Paying attention to the road, Winston didn't notice the gleam in Jessica's eye or the insistent tone in her voice. "Sure," he said, casually, "if he's not asleep. They got in pretty late last night."

Jessica wasn't about to be deterred by Marty's being tired. She had been through too much hardship and spent too many hours with Winston to make concessions simply because Marty needed a nap. "I've got to meet him," she repeated.

Winston glanced over at her. "Hey, what's the big deal about meeting Marty?"

Now Jessica was afraid she'd gone too far. She didn't want to be obvious about her plan. "I guess your mother told my mom he was coming to visit. She told me to say hello for her," Jessica said, the lie rolling easily off her tongue.

Winston pulled into his driveway. "That's nice of you, Jess," he said.

But once they were inside the house, Marty was nowhere to be seen. Mrs. Egbert was very much in evidence, however, and she seemed to be a bit distraught. "Oh, Winston, I'm so glad you're home."

"What's up?" he asked.

"I'm having that cocktail party for Marty and Jane tonight, and the caterer's truck broke down. They can't deliver, so I have to pick up the hors d'oeuvres. Can you drive me over and help carry the food?"

"Sure. Do you want to go right now?"

"Yes, we've got to get there before they close." Now her eye fell on Jessica. "Jessica, dear, I'm sorry to interrupt your study plans. Do you want to come with us? Of course, you can stay here if you like. We shouldn't be too long."

Jessica saw this as her golden opportunity. If she stayed there, she might get to talk to Marty alone. "I think I'll just wait here and get going on our paper, Mrs. Egbert," she said politely. "We've still got a lot to do."

"Fine, fine," said Mrs. Egbert. She looked at her watch. "Let's go, Winston. We haven't got much time."

The moment Winston and his mother left the house, Jessica started snooping around, looking for Marty. She went first to the backyard, where she thought he might be sunning himself, but he wasn't there. Nor was he in the kitchen or family room. Just when she had concluded he was tucked away in one of the bedrooms, having a nap, she bumped into him as he walked around the corner of the hallway. Barefoot and wearing jeans and a shirt, Marty hardly looked like an important movie director. Still the normally ebullient Jessica was dumbstruck just to be in the presence of this middle-aged man with graying blond hair.

"Hello." Marty smiled at her. "Who might you be?"

"Jessica Wakefield," she stammered.

"Well, Jessica Wakefield, where is everybody?" he asked pleasantly.

"They've gone to the caterers."

"Would you know where they keep the coffee around here? I need to wake myself up."

"I think I can find it," she said, flashing him a brilliant smile. She led him into the kitchen.

"I'm Marty Davis, by the way," he introduced himself as he filled the kettle with water. "I assume you're a friend of Winston's?"

"Yes. Winston and I are very good friends." She started to search through the cupboard and found the coffee a moment later.

They made small talk for a few minutes while Marty waited for the water to boil. Finally Jessica got up the courage to ask a pointed question. "So, Mr. Davis, I hear you're in a pretty interesting line of work."

"Well, I think so. And call me Marty, please." He poured water into a cup and added a spoonful of instant coffee. "Would you like some?"

Jessica shook her head. "No, thanks. Do you live in Los Angeles?" she asked.

"No, I live in San Francisco, but my work takes me to L.A. a lot. As a matter of fact, I'm about to start a new project there," he told her pleasantly.

"Really?" Jessica said enthusiastically. "I'd like to hear all about it. That is, if you want to talk about it," she added quickly.

"I don't know . . ." Marty said hesitantly.

"I hear you're very good," Jessica said. "I have some career aspirations in that direction myself."

"You do?" Marty sipped his drink. "I must say I like discussing my work with someone who's interested. Tell you what, I've got to do some things around here and get ready for that party Sharon is throwing tonight. Why don't you come over on Saturday. I'll show you the concept, and we can talk about it."

"Terrific," Jessica declared, beaming. "Listen, Mr. Davis—"

"Marty."

"Right. I just remembered, there's something I have to do at home. Will you tell Winston that I had to leave and I'll see him tomorrow?"

"Sure thing," Marty answered.

"Thanks, thanks for everything."

"You're welcome, Jessica."

Jessica went to the entrance hall to collect her books. She decided to go over to the Dairi Burger to see if she could catch a ride home with someone. There was no need to hang around the Egberts' any longer. Her mission had been accomplished.

Eleven

Cara went to her closet and searched through the dresses hanging there. This was going to be a very special night, and she wanted to look perfect. Not only was it her birthday, but she was going out on a date with Steven Wakefield. What more could she want?

Since their picnic at the zoo the weekend before, Steven had called her twice, and on Wednesday, after his classes, he had driven the short distance to Sweet Valley just to visit her. He hadn't even stopped in to see his family. After they spent the evening watching television, he had gone right back to campus.

Since her mom had been working late that evening, they'd had the apartment to themselves. But there hadn't been the least hint of romance. Both times Steven had been friendly but reserved. That was all right with Cara, though. Just spending time with Steven was enough for now.

It was on Wednesday that Steven had noticed Cara's calendar with her birthday circled in red. At first he just wished her a happy birthday. But before he left he asked if she would like to celebrate by going out to dinner with him. Steven had told her to pick the spot. He hadn't said anything specific about where he wanted to go, but Cara thought an out-of-the-way place would be best. She had decided, therefore, to make reservations at the Valley Inn. It was a charming old restaurant just outside of town. It was unlikely that any of their friends would see them there.

Cara looked through her closet one more time and finally chose a soft blue-and-white print dress that showed off her tanned complexion. She pulled her hair up into a topknot and put on the pearl earrings her parents had given her for Christmas. Her mind flew back to that occasion only months ago. The family had been happy then, or at least it had seemed so at the time. *Well, there's no point in thinking about that now*, she chided herself. *I've got a wonderful evening ahead with a boy I've always liked.* The future looked very bright indeed.

Cara was putting on some perfume when she

heard the door bell ring. She checked the mirror one more time, took a deep breath, and went to answer it.

"Hello, Cara," Steven greeted her. In his blue blazer, crisp white shirt, and gray flannel slacks, he looked even more handsome than usual.

"Hi, Steve," she said almost shyly. "Come in."

"You look lovely," he said.

"Thanks." Cara smiled. "Why don't you sit down for a while. I made reservations for seven-thirty, and it's a little before seven now."

"Fine," Steven agreed, settling himself on the love seat. "That will give you time to open your gift."

Cara had been so busy admiring Steven, she hadn't noticed the package he was carrying.

"Oh, Steve, you shouldn't have."

"What's a birthday without a present?" he said, handing it to her. "It's just something I thought you might like. I wrapped it myself," he apologized.

Cara looked more closely at the present. It was wrapped in pink-and-white paper and tied with a festive ribbon. She was touched that Steven had gone to so much trouble.

"Aren't you going to open it?" he asked.

"Of course I am." She sat down in the arm-chair next to him and carefully began to untie the ribbon.

"Why don't you just tear it off?"

"Absolutely not," she declared. "I'm going to take the same care in opening it that you put into wrapping it."

Steven gave her a pleased look. "OK, take your time."

After she got the ribbon off, she read the card. "Happy birthday to someone nice," it read.

The present itself was a big hit, a mystery novel by one of Cara's favorite authors. "Oh, good," she exclaimed.

"It's his latest. It just arrived in the bookstores."

"I know. I read a review in the paper, and I've been dying to read it. Thank you, Steve." She wanted to kiss him, but one glance at Steven told her she shouldn't. Instead she just smiled and said it was nice of him to think of her.

"Can I get you something to drink?" she asked after a moment.

"No, thanks." He looked at his watch. "Maybe we should get going. It was starting to rain when I came in, and I don't want to get tied up in traffic."

"Oh, maybe I should get my raincoat," Cara said, heading toward the hall.

"By the way," Steven called to her, "where are we going?"

Cara's muffled voice came back to him from the closet. "The Valley Inn."

Fortunately Cara could not see Steven's reaction to her announcement. He paled, and his eyes took on a haunted look. *The Valley Inn*, he thought. That was the restaurant he and Tricia had gone to before she became too sick to leave the house. A flood of memories washed over him: Tricia, frail but more beautiful than ever, dancing in his arms; asking the band to play Tricia's favorite old song, "Always"; whispering the lyrics in her ear as they moved to the music. The last place in the world Steven wanted to go was the Valley Inn.

"Steve." Steven looked up to see Cara standing in front of him, her raincoat on. Obviously this was not the first time she had called him. "Didn't you want to leave now?"

He averted his eyes from her gaze. Cara looked so beautiful, and she had been so excited and hopeful when he had walked through the door. Now her face wore a worried expression, as if she were wondering what she had done to change his mood. Steven didn't want to hurt her again. He would just put aside his own feelings and go on with the date as though nothing were wrong.

"I'm all set," he said, opening the door for her. It had stopped raining, and the air outside smelled fresh and new. Cara was so energetic and cheerful on the ride to the Valley Inn that

Steven's tension began to fade. Maybe going there wouldn't be so bad after all.

There were, however, a shaky couple of minutes as they stood at the entrance to the dining room, waiting for the maître d'hôtel to show them to their table. The last time Steven had looked out across the dining room, Tricia had been on his arm. Fortunately, he and Cara were soon shown to a table on the end of the room opposite where he had been with Tricia.

"This place is lovely," Cara said, looking at the snow-white table linens and the fresh flowers on every table. In a corner, a band was playing romantic old songs.

"Yes, it is," Steven replied wistfully.

"Have you ever been here before?" Cara asked.

"I—I was here with my family once." That was the truth. Steven and the twins had taken their parents there several years before for an anniversary celebration. Before Steven could decide whether to say anything about Tricia, a waiter came over and handed them large white dinner menus.

They both decided to have prime rib, tossed green salad, and a baked potato. During the meal Steven kept the conversation focused on Cara and what she had been up to lately. Like Jessica, Cara was on the Sweet Valley High cheerleading squad. Happily she described some of their latest practice sessions. Then she and Steven laughed and told stories about some of the teachers they had both had at school.

Cara giggled. "You mean Mrs. Ray used to frighten a big guy like you?"

"Heck, yes," Steven declared. "She may have looked like a tiny little thing, but if you didn't know how to conjugate those Spanish verbs, you were as good as dead. I'd rather mess with a heavyweight boxer than old Mrs. Ray."

Cara nodded and told Steven about the time she had left her homework in the cafeteria. "When I got to class and realized I didn't have it with me, I knew I must have thrown it out with my lunch, by accident. I rushed downstairs and started pawing through the trash cans, looking for it. Doing that was better than telling Mrs. Ray I didn't have the assignment."

Steven's mind drifted away from Cara for a moment. Having dinner in the Valley Inn with someone other than Tricia wasn't as difficult as he'd thought it would be. At first being there had been hard, but sitting across from Cara was taking the sting out of it. By the time the waiter brought dessert, cherry pie and ice cream, Steven was at ease.

"Oh, I'm sorry," Steven said suddenly, sitting up straight.

"Why, what did you do?" Cara asked, perplexed.

"I should have told the waiter it was your birthday. Then he could have brought you a special piece of birthday cake."

"And have the whole restaurant sing 'Happy Birthday' to me? No, thanks." Cara shook her head. "I'm glad you didn't."

"Would that have embarrassed you?"

"It would have terrified me. It's funny. At one time I always wanted to be the center of attention. Now I prefer to stay out of the spotlight."

"I've got an idea, Cara. Since you don't like to stand out, why don't we go out to that nice, crowded dance floor?"

"Why not?" Cara agreed.

Steven got up, went over to Cara's side of the table, and pulled out her chair. "Shall we, Ms. Walker?"

The band was playing a slow, romantic song, and even though Steven held Cara loosely in his arms, it was hard to deny she was stirring warm feelings inside him.

"This is a beautiful song," Cara said, looking up at him.

"Lovely, just like the girl I'm with."

The music ended, and Cara started back toward their table.

"Not so fast! How about another one?" Steven said, pulling her back to him.

"OK," Cara answered, pleased that Steven wanted to dance some more.

116

As the band struck up the introduction to the next song, Steven took Cara in his arms once more. But when the band went into the melody, his back stiffened.

"*Always*"! The band was playing the song Tricia had loved so much! Suddenly the room seemed suffocatingly hot, and Steven felt as though he couldn't breathe.

Cara quickly noticed his distress. "Steven, what's wrong? Are you ill?"

He tried to cover up. "No, I feel fine," he said. But there was a sick feeling in his stomach and a sick feeling in his heart. How could he dance to this song with another girl in his arms? It was the ultimate disloyalty. The two of them were barely moving now, and Steven was hardly aware of Cara. The only thing he could hear was that song, "Always."

Tricia believed I knew the meaning of that word, Steven thought to himself bitterly, *but I guess I don't*.

Cara looked up at Steven's pale face. "Can't you tell me what's wrong?"

He focused on her and shook his head. No, he couldn't—he didn't want to explain. All he wanted was to get away from there and leave the haunting music behind. Cara's face began to swim before his eyes, and he felt dizzy. He stopped dancing and stood rooted to the spot, but his voice was agitated. "No, Cara, I, uh—Cara, I'm sorry. I have to go." With those words he left her standing alone on the dance floor and dashed away. Heads turned, and Cara saw Steven stop at the table, pull out some money, toss it on the table, and rush out the door.

Feeling as if she were about to die of embarrassment, Cara made her way back. The waiter had already left the check, so Cara had only to pay with the money Steven had left, gather her things, and leave. She used the public telephone in the reception area to call a taxi. Her face now a stormy mask, Cara sat on a bench outside the Valley Inn and waited for her cab to arrive.

As Cara put her key in the door of her apartment, she could hear the telephone ringing, but she didn't rush to get inside. She was in no mood to speak to anyone. As she entered the apartment, the phone stopped ringing. Cara felt more weary than ever before in her life. She removed her shoes and lay down on the living-room couch. She tried not to think about anything. She didn't want to think. Then the phone started to ring again. She looked at it, willing it to stop. Finally she roused herself to answer it.

"Hello," she said tentatively.

"Cara, it's me."

There was no need for Steven to identify himself. Cara knew who was on the other end of the phone, but she didn't say a word.

"Are you there?" he asked plaintively.

"Yes."

"Cara, I'm so sorry. Please let me explain."

When Cara again said nothing, Steven plunged ahead. "I was having a wonderful time, really I was, but I didn't want to tell you that the Valley Inn was where Tricia and I spent our last date."

"You should have told me," Cara said flatly after a moment's thought. "It could have saved us both a lot of heartache."

"It didn't bother me that much," Steven insisted. "Not after we started having such a good time."

"Then what went wrong?" Cara asked unemotionally.

"It was the song the band was playing, 'Always.' That song was Tricia's favorite. I felt awful hearing it while I was holding someone else in my arms." Steven waited a moment for Cara to say something. He almost hoped she would be angry with him, but when she remained quiet, he rushed on. "I'm sorry, Cara. It was unforgiveable of me to leave you there alone. Did you get home all right?" he asked with embarrassment.

"Yes, I called a cab," she said simply.

After another pause, Steven said, "Cara, what can I do to make this up to you?"

Cara considered the question and then answered sadly. "Steve, I like you very much. You know I do. But you're tied to Tricia in a way that I think is unhealthy for any relationship of ours. Tell me the truth, Steve. You don't feel free to see other girls, do you?"

"Not really," he admitted.

"I'm sorry for that, Steven. I am. But I can't compete with a ghost. And the truth is, I don't even want to."

"Cara, I wish I could have one more chance."

"I'd like to help you get through this. Are you ready for me to do that?" she said cautiously.

Steven knew it was important to give Cara an honest answer to that question. Unfortunately, it would make neither of them happy. "I wish I were, Cara."

"But you're not."

"No. I'm not," Steven answered quietly.

Twelve

It was Saturday, and Jessica was ready for her conference with Marty Davis. She had waited patiently all week. Now her chance at movie stardom was only hours away. But Jessica didn't want the Egberts hanging around while she talked to Marty. She wanted to see him alone.

The first step in arranging her visit was to call the Egbert house to see who was going to be home. Jessica dialed the Egberts' number.

Winston picked up the phone on the second ring. "Egbert Summer Home. Some are home. Some are not," he sang out.

Jessica rolled her eyes. "Very amusing, Winston. It's Jessica. Listen, I'm calling to see when we can get together today."

"This morning's no good. My mother and I are going out with Aunt Jane. Uncle Marty will be the only one home."

Jessica's eyes grew wide. "Oh, is that so? You know, I'm going to be in your neighborhood in a little while. I just may wander over to your house and get started. You have most of the research materials there."

"If that's what you want to do. We should be back by one or so."

"Fine, Winston. I'll see you then."

Perfect, Jessica thought as she put down the phone.

She walked into the kitchen buoyed by her triumph. She was taken aback by the sight of her downcast mother slowly stirring her cup of coffee. Alice Wakefield's normally youthful face seemed older and weary.

"Mom, what's the problem?"

"I guess you haven't seen Steve this morning."

Jessica sat down beside her. "No, I haven't."

Elizabeth walked in and joined her sister and mother. "I did. I don't understand. What could have happened to upset him so? Everything's been going so well for him this last week."

"Are you sure something's wrong?" Jessica persisted.

"He was pacing all last night," Mrs. Wakefield informed her. "I got up around three, and he was just sitting in the den. He had made a fire and was staring into it. I told him I had heard him walking around, and I asked if there was anything I could do. He told me to leave him alone."

"Boy, that doesn't sound like Steve," Jessica said. "Could he and Cara have had a fight?"

"I don't know," Elizabeth told her. "He left with Betsy this morning."

"Betsy! So where does that leave Cara?"

"Steven's terribly unstable right now," Mrs. Wakefield said. "I don't know how long he can go on this way."

"Something's got to turn him around, but what can that be?" Elizabeth asked, distressed.

Jessica was upset by the turn in her brother's situation as well, but he would have to wait. After all, she had plans for the day. "Listen, I've got to go. I'll talk to you later about what's happening to Steve." She gave her mother a kiss on the top of the head before she left the kitchen.

On the way to Winston's, Jessica toyed with the idea of dropping by to see Cara. She finally decided it would be a waste of time since her friend had been so closemouthed lately. She would just go to Winston's as planned and worry about Steven later. Maybe he'd cheer up when she came home with the exciting news she was going to star in a new movie.

Jessica was practically bursting with excitement as she climbed the steps to Winston's front door. When no one answered after a few rings, she went around the house to see if Marty was in the backyard. Sure enough, he was sitting on a green lounge chair, leafing through a thick volume bound with blue paper covers. *That must be the script*, Jessica said to herself, moving quickly toward the part of the yard where Marty was seated. When he looked up, Jessica gave him her most winning smile.

"Jessica, how are you?"

"Couldn't be better. What have you got there?" she asked coyly.

"Come sit here." He patted the chair next to him. "This is the project I mentioned."

Jessica took a seat and leaned over to look at the sizable manuscript. "I can't wait to see this," she said enthusiastically.

He handed her the massive volume. "Well, go to it."

"This is one piece of reading I won't mind doing," Jessica told him.

"You're not going to read the whole thing, are you?" Marty asked, startled.

"You don't think I should?"

"I think it would be better to begin with the part that interests you."

Aha! So there was a part in this film for her, Jessica thought. Marty must already have decided to cast her.

"I have a better idea," Jessica said. "Why don't you just tell me the story?"

Marty threw his head back and laughed as though he had just heard the funniest joke in the world. "Tell you the story! Oh, that's great."

It is? Jessica wondered.

"Let's see, I think I can do that. This is the story of a man who wants to find the best routes to move garbage out of Los Angeles."

"Garbage?" Jessica said weakly. "Garbage isn't a topic with much appeal, is it?"

"Probably not. But we're lucky we like it, aren't we?" he responded, giving her a little wink.

Jessica seriously doubted that a movie about garbage would ever be a success. Still, Marty was a well-respected Hollywood director, and probably knew better. But maybe he was just eccentric. Certainly Winston was strange. It might just run in the family.

"Why don't I just take a look for myself," Jessica said after a troubled pause. Maybe she could get some clue about what was happening from the script.

"Of course," Marty said. "Take your time." He settled back in his chair and closed his eyes.

The blue paper cover was blank. When Jessica turned to the title page, however, she received the shock of her life. "Strategies for Waste Disposal in Los Angeles County," it read. Was this

125

some sort of horrible joke? she wondered. No, the table of contents listing the different methods of garbage removal seemed quite clear and to the point. She hurriedly looked over the introduction. It was a letter to the Los Angeles Board of County Commissioners, and it was signed by Martin Davis, civil engineer.

"You're a civil engineer?" Jessica said carefully.

Marty opened his eyes and sat up. Now it was his turn to be surprised. "You knew that, didn't you?"

"I wasn't sure of your exact title," Jessica said.

"You're going to have to get your master's degree in engineering, too, you know. After you get a bachelor's in math or one of the sciences. Are you good in those subjects?"

"My chemistry teacher tells me I should be in a class by myself." This was true. She was always talking and passing notes in Mr. Russo's class. One day he commented that she should be in a room alone, where she couldn't bother any of the other students.

"That's important," Marty said. "Anyway, I'm sure you will find this very rewarding work. Why don't we just go over some of the report together now?"

For a moment Jessica thought she should apologize for wasting Marty's time and excuse herself, but she was too mortified to do that. Instead she sat in the hot sun for an hour, listening to Marty discuss the many ways of moving garbage out of Los Angeles. Finally, she was saved by Winston's arrival. She could never have imagined being so happy to see Winston Egbert.

After thanking Marty for his time, Jessica followed Winston into the kitchen.

"Winston, could I have something cold to drink?" she asked. "I feel like the top of my head is coming off."

"Sure," Winston said agreeably, going to the refrigerator. He poured her a glass of lemonade. "I don't understand, Jess," he said a moment later. "Why were you and Uncle Marty sitting around discussing his report?"

"I don't know." She waved her hand vaguely. "It seemed like a good idea at the time."

"Yeah, Uncle Marty is a pretty interesting guy. It's a shame you couldn't meet his brother, Phil."

Jessica raised her head wearily. "Phil?"

"Phil Davis. You must have heard of him. He's a famous movie director. He's made all kinds of terrific films. He does a lot of movies for teenagers."

Jessica could barely force the words out. "Was he supposed to come, too?"

"Yeah, but he had to cancel at the last minute. He needed to finish up shooting in London. He felt terrible about it."

127

"I can see where that might make someone feel bad," Jessica agreed.

"So, are you ready to get going?"

"I don't think so, Winston. I think I just want to go home. I'm not feeling very well."

"That's too bad. Don't you even want to stay for lunch?" Winston asked. "My mother is making Tuna Surprise."

Jessica got up and headed toward the door. "No, thanks, Winston. I've had quite enough surprises for one day."

Thirteen

"So you see, Liz, the evening just turned into a disaster."

Steven and Elizabeth were riding in Steven's yellow Volkswagen. Elizabeth was headed for the Dairi Burger to meet Jessica, and Steven had insisted on driving her so he could confide in her about the previous night.

Elizabeth sighed. Steven had been a big help to her lately in her problems with Todd. She wanted to offer him the same kind of support, but she wasn't sure she knew how.

"I'm sure if you explained the whole thing to Cara—" Elizabeth began tentatively.

"I told you I tried," Steven broke in. "What's the point? Like I told Cara, I just don't feel I'm ready to start over again. And right now it seems as though maybe I never will be."

"Oh, Steve, don't say that. It's just taking longer than you thought it would."

Steven pulled into a parking space in front of the Dairi Burger and turned off the ignition. He turned to look at his sister, whose aqua eyes were as troubled as his own. "Cara's a sweet kid. She's like Trish in a lot of ways. And she's vulnerable, too, because she's been hurt recently. And I just find myself adding more to that hurt."

Elizabeth was at a loss for words. Her heart ached for Steven. "Where are you going now?"

"I thought I'd go over and see Betsy."

She wasn't sure how to tell Steven that she didn't think that sounded like a good idea. "Well, if you think it will make you feel better," she said doubtfully.

"It will. She was supposed to show me some more pictures of Tricia when she was a kid. Maybe they turned up."

It sounded like a depressing way to spend the afternoon, but apparently Steven didn't think so. She leaned over to kiss him, once again wishing she could do more. "Take care of yourself, Steve," she said, getting out of the car. She stood on the curb for a moment, watching him pull away. There had to be something she could do. But what? She racked her brain, but no solution presented itself. Slowly she walked into the

Dairi Burger, where she spotted Jessica sitting in a corner booth, a crestfallen expression on her face.

"How's it going?" Elizabeth asked, sliding into the booth.

"Terrible."

"You didn't sound very happy when you called. Are you ready to talk about it?"

Jessica shook her head. "It's too humiliating."

"Well, then, let's go up and order some lunch. My treat," Elizabeth coaxed.

"I'm too upset to eat."

"Then just walk up to the counter and keep me company."

"All right," Jessica agreed reluctantly.

The twins made their way through the throng in front of the counter to the spot where orders were placed. John Doherty, one of the owners of the Dairi Burger, looked up to take their order. "What can I get you two?"

"I'll have a hamburger, small fries, and a root beer," Elizabeth said, sneaking a peek at Jessica, who was standing with her head down.

"Excuse me. What about you?" Doherty asked Jessica when she made no effort to give her order.

"Nothing for me," she said with an exaggerated sigh.

"Come on," Elizabeth urged. "You've got to eat something."

"You're paying, Liz?"

Her sister nodded.

"Then I guess I could force something down. A hamburger," she said to Mr. Doherty. "And a vanilla milkshake," she added a moment later. "To soothe my stomach," she informed her sister.

"That's it?" John said, pencil poised.

"Oh, you might as well give me some french fries."

"Anything else?" he asked one more time.

"Of course not," Jessica answered indignantly. "I'm not that hungry."

When the girls got back to their table, Elizabeth turned her attention once again to Jessica. "All right, now what's going on here? Spill it."

And Jessica did. She told her twin the whole story, from beginning to end. "So," she finished, "there it is, the terrible tale of how I was tricked and betrayed by the Egbert family."

That theatrical flourish was too much, even for Elizabeth. "Come on, Jessica, face facts. The only person who did any tricking was you."

Jessica put on her saddest expression. "All right, I admit it. Maybe I wasn't totally honest, but I paid for it, didn't I? No movie job, no Academy Award, and the whole school is laughing about Winston Egbert and me. People think I'm *interested* in him."

"Winston's a perfectly nice guy, Jessica, and

everyone in the school thinks so except you and some of your snobby friends," Elizabeth declared staunchly.

Now it was time for Jessica's final confession. "Then you won't mind that I told a few people I was just being nice to him so I could put in a good word for you?" Jessica asked hopefully.

"Oh, Jessica!" Elizabeth burst into laughter. "No, it doesn't matter. It's just another rumor. Everyone will forget all about it soon."

John brought over their order. Without a moment's hesitation, Jessica hungrily dived into hers.

"So, is the real movie director ever coming to town?" Elizabeth asked, taking a smaller bite of her burger.

"Who knows? Who cares?" Jessica said, popping a french fry into her mouth. Then she looked at Elizabeth with gleaming eyes. "Wait—I do."

Elizabeth groaned.

"Why, I've already laid the groundwork with the Egberts, haven't I? Phil Davis is sure to show up in Sweet Valley one of these days, and I want to be ready when he comes."

"Be ready? How?" Elizabeth asked wearily.

"I have to stay on good terms with his favorite nephew, of course."

"But you just said . . ."

Jessica gulped down another bite of hamburger and sipped her shake. "Listen, Liz, wait for me here, will you? Lila just came in, and I want to ask her something." With that, she dashed away and left Elizabeth sitting alone.

Elizabeth wasn't surprised at her sister's manipulations. Nor did she worry too much about her. Jessica could take care of herself. If only she could say the same for Steven.

It was awful that Steven was clinging so fiercely to Tricia's memory. Tricia hadn't wanted it to be that way. Elizabeth knew that for a fact. If only there were a way to make Steven and Betsy realize it.

Wait, Elizabeth thought to herself, *I think I know how to do just that.*

Fourteen

As Elizabeth turned the Fiat onto Wentworth Avenue, the neighborhood began to get worse. Trash littered the sidewalk, and pieces of broken glass sparkled in the sun. This did not seem at all like the Sweet Valley Elizabeth knew and loved.

She drove slowly down the street, looking for the address of Betsy Martin's house. When she found it, she was dismayed to see that it was one of the worst-looking homes on the block. The house was badly in need of paint, and the lawn was brown and overgrown with weeds. A broken swing hung on the front porch.

Elizabeth parked the car, looked around, and just sat inside. She wanted to make sure Steven's car wasn't nearby. In many ways Steven's moods were shaped by Betsy. Yet Elizabeth knew that Betsy wasn't hurting Steven on purpose. She probably thought she was giving Steven good advice. It was up to Elizabeth to show Betsy she was wrong. Fortunately she knew a secret that would help her to do just that.

Elizabeth got out of the car and resolutely walked up the sagging steps. When the bell didn't work, she knocked loudly.

The door opened a crack, and Elizabeth could see Betsy's hazel eyes peering out. "Elizabeth!" she exclaimed in a shocked voice. Then she opened the door a little wider. "What are you doing here?"

"Betsy," insisted Elizabeth, "it's important that I see you. I wouldn't have come here if it wasn't."

Betsy silently opened the door and led her inside.

Elizabeth and Betsy walked into the small, neat living room. Clean, faded curtains hung from the windows, and a crocheted afghan covered the back of a rocking chair. A few of Tricia's watercolors hung on the wall, though their bright shades served only to emphasize the dinginess of the walls.

Elizabeth sat down in the rocking chair and gestured to the seat next to her. "Come, sit down, Betsy. Let's talk."

Betsy warily sat down in the chair.

"Betsy," Elizabeth began, "we got to be pretty good friends when you stayed with us."

Betsy's hard expression melted. Her mind flew back, and she remembered all the nice things Elizabeth had done for her while she was a guest in the Wakefield home after Tricia's death. "We're more than friends," Betsy replied. "You really helped me get myself together."

"I didn't bring this up so you could thank me, Betsy. I just wanted to remind you I'm not your enemy."

Betsy looked away. "I guess I have been feeling that you and Jessica aren't very happy about the time I spend with Steve."

"It's not the time, Betsy. It's just that you two always spend so much of it talking about Tricia."

Betsy grew indignant. "And why shouldn't we? She was the most important person in the world to both of us."

"I know she was, but now I want to tell you about some things that were important to her: two promises."

"Promises?" Betsy asked curiously.

"Yes, you know about one of them. While she was dying, Tricia made Steve promise to take care of you."

Betsy flushed. "Why are you bringing that up, Liz? It caused all kinds of problems."

"Yes," Elizabeth agreed, "because Steve thought that meant taking total responsibility for

137

your life. But it was a misunderstanding that needed to get sorted out, which it finally was."

"What was the other promise?"

"You don't know about this one. It was a promise I made to Tricia at her request. And later I broke it on purpose. I thought I was doing the right thing at the time. Now, I'm not so sure."

"Tell me about it," Betsy implored.

Elizabeth settled back to tell the story. "You see, when Tricia discovered she had leukemia, she decided not to tell Steve she was sick. She just broke up with him and pretended she wasn't interested in him anymore."

"Why did she do that?"

"She figured that eventually it would be less painful for him, because by the time she died, he'd be over her."

"I remember when they broke up." Betsy got up and paced the well-worn carpet. "Tricia was so miserable then, but I was too drunk or stoned to ask just what was going on."

"Then I found out Tricia was terminally ill," Elizabeth continued, "and she made me promise not to tell Steve. I kept that promise for a while, but finally I decided they would both be happier spending her final weeks together. So I told Steve the truth."

Betsy stopped walking back and forth and sat back down. "That final time they had together was beautiful. Telling Steve was the right thing to do."

Elizabeth looked at her steadily. "Was it? I thought so once. Now, I think I made a dreadful mistake."

"But why?" Betsy cried.

"Because Tricia was right. If I had kept that promise, Steve would have been over her already. Now he's suffering more and more."

For a second Betsy stared at Elizabeth with large, uncomprehending eyes. Then realization swept over her face. "You think I'm responsible for that, don't you?"

"Yes, in part, Betsy. I'm afraid you are."

Tears began to spill down Betsy's cheeks. "How could you think I would do anything to hurt Steve?"

"I don't think you would—intentionally," Elizabeth assured her, "but I think that's what has happened. Steve can't start looking forward to the future because you keep asking him to dwell on the past."

"I never thought of it that way. I just feel this awesome responsibility to keep Tricia's memory alive. And the only people who can do that are Steven and me."

"Yes, Betsy, but it's easy for you to hold Tricia close and go on with your life. There's no conflict for you to have your memories of Tricia and a relationship with Jason as well. But it's much more complicated for Steve."

"I see what you mean," Betsy said slowly. "Every time he tried to bring Cara into his life, I was right there, insisting he should be thinking about Tricia."

Before speaking, Elizabeth thought over her next question carefully. "Everyone wants to remember someone who's gone, Betsy, but you're still so tied to Tricia. Why is that?"

"Can't you guess, Liz?" Betsy asked, her voice rising.

"Why don't you tell me."

"I'm trying to be a good sister to Tricia now that she's gone, because I was such a terrible one while she was alive." With that confession, Betsy broke down and cried.

Elizabeth stood up and put her arms around Betsy's shoulders. It took a few moments for Betsy to compose herself. Then she let her words spill out. "We were a pretty normal family until my mother got sick and died. Then everything started falling apart. My dad began drinking. When I was in my early teens, I started drinking, too. We were both trying to block things out. Tricia was the strong one, always trying to take care of us. But she needed someone to take care of her, too. I was never there for her."

"Tricia knew how much you loved her," Elizabeth interrupted.

"Sure she did. That's what made her such a wonderful sister. She was sweet and forgiving. She was always trying to get me to stay off the booze and the drugs and get myself together."

"And you've done that," Elizabeth said encouragingly. "Your sister would be proud."

"Oh, yes, I did it. Just a little too late, that's all. Just like I got to the hospital too late to see Tricia before she died." Betsy's voice cracked with remorse.

"Betsy, you're very lucky," Elizabeth began. "You have an opportunity not many people get. You can still grant your sister her last wish."

"I can?" Betsy said hopefully.

"You know now that Tricia wanted to set Steve free so that he could go on with his life."

"Yes, I realize that."

"Then it's up to you to make him believe that. We've all talked to him until we're blue in the face."

"So you want me to call him," Betsy said, getting up eagerly. "I can do that right now."

"There's one catch." Elizabeth sighed. "I'm not sure just words will convince him at this point. He's so mixed up. And he's hurt Cara badly. I don't know if those two will ever find their way back together."

Betsy sank back down in her seat. Her confusion cleared, and she spoke with determination. "This situation is mostly my fault. If I messed

141

things up, then I should be able to fix them again."

"But how?" Elizabeth asked.

"I've got to do something so that Steve will know that he has to face the future. That it's what both Tricia and I want."

"That's a pretty tall order," Elizabeth told her.

Betsy flashed Elizabeth a mysterious smile. "Yes, it is," she said, "but I think I know just what to do."

Fifteen

Dusk was falling as Steven Wakefield paced under the Romanesque clock outside Sweet Valley High. He checked his watch. It was seven o'clock.

Steven thought back to the strange message his mother had left on his desk. He had been out riding his bicycle, trying to clear his mind. When he'd gotten home, everyone was gone, so he went upstairs to look where his family usually left him notes and reminders. This one said, "We've gone out to dinner. There's food in the fridge if you want it. Don't forget to meet your friend under the clock at Sweet Valley High at 7:00." Steven had racked his brain, trying to think of whom he had set up an appointment

143

with. No one came to mind. Still it must be important because his mother had underlined the words "Don't forget."

Steven had arrived ten minutes early, just to make sure he didn't miss his mysterious appointment, but he had seen no one except young Teddy Collins. Teddy was Roger Collins's six-year-old son, and since their house was near the campus, Teddy often rode his bicycle on the wide lawn. Teddy and Steven were old buddies, and the boy had given him a friendly wave when Steven walked by.

Steven checked his watch again. It was five after seven. This was silly. Maybe someone was playing a joke on him. If he was still alone in five minutes, Steven decided, he was just going to leave.

Just then, he heard a rustling noise behind him. He turned to see Cara Walker step out of the shadows. Surprise registered on Cara's face, but she couldn't be any more surprised than he was.

They looked uncertainly at each other.

"Cara, what are you doing here?" Steven asked.

Cara became indignant at his tone. "I was going to ask you the same thing."

"My mother left me a message to meet someone here," he told her.

"That's funny," Cara said slowly. "I got a

144

message from my mother that said the same thing. I have it right here." She handed him the crumpled note, and Steven glanced at it. Sure enough, the note instructed Cara to be at school, under the clock at seven.

"So this wasn't your doing?" Steven asked.

"Hardly," Cara said icily.

"I didn't mean it like that, Cara. I'm glad to have a chance to talk to you alone."

Cara turned away from him. "Steve, I think we've hurt each other enough. Let's not make the whole thing worse."

They stood together awkwardly for a moment, neither of them saying a word.

"I wonder who set this up?" Steven finally asked.

Cara turned back toward him. "Probably one of the twins. Maybe Jessica."

"I don't know. My mom wouldn't go along with something like this, I don't think."

"My mother would have said in the message if it was Jessica who called. She knows her voice very well."

They lapsed into silence. Then Steven went over to Cara and put his arm around her shoulder. "As long as someone went to this much trouble, don't you think we should at least try to straighten things out?"

The warmth of Steven's arm against her body melted Cara's icy exterior. "All right, but I don't really think there's much to say. You've already admitted to me that you don't feel free to date."

Just then Teddy Collins came riding up near them. "Steve, Cara," he called. "Come here."

"Why, what's wrong?" Steven asked.

"I've got something for you."

Steven and Cara turned to each other. What could Teddy Collins possibly have for them? "It must be something he found," Cara concluded. "We might as well humor him."

They walked over to him and were surprised to see him holding two identical small packages in his hand. They were beautifully wrapped, and one had a card that was labeled "Steven," while the other read "Cara."

"Where did you get these, Teddy?" Steven demanded.

"I'm not supposed to tell, so I won't," he said proudly.

"Did you get them from a stranger?" Cara asked with concern. "You know you're not supposed to talk to people you don't know."

"No," Teddy said scornfully. "I knew 'em."

"More than one," Steven said in an undertone to Cara. "The plot thickens. Well, young man, hand them over. They've got our names on them."

"Stev-en," Teddy read the name carefully and solemnly gave Steve his. "Cara," he said, smiling now that his important task was ended.

"Thanks," Steven and Cara chorused. They waved as Teddy rode away.

Steven and Cara sat down on the stairs of the school. "Shall we?" Steven asked.

"I can't wait to see what this is all about," Cara answered, tearing into hers.

They could not have been more surprised when the packages were opened. Cara held in her hand a beautifully drawn pencil sketch of Steven. It captured perfectly his handsome likeness and good nature. In Steven's hand there was a portrait of Cara, which was every bit as beautiful as the girl.

"Only one person could have done these," Steven said slowly. "Betsy Martin."

"But why would she?" Cara asked, confused. "She was the one who didn't think we should be together."

There was excitement in Steven's eyes now, and his voice shook with happiness. "Don't you see? She's changed her mind." Steven felt a great relief sweep over him. Then Cara noticed a piece of paper that had fallen to the ground. "Look, Steve, I think there was a note in yours."

Steven bent over to pick it up. "Yes, it's a note from Betsy." He read it aloud.

Dear Steve,

I have finally come to realize what Tricia knew long ago: a wonderful person like you should be looking toward his future, not his past. You made my sister so happy while she was alive. Now it's time for you to bring your kindness and affection to someone else. Do what Trish wanted, Steve: embrace life and all the beautiful things it has to offer.

Fondly,
Betsy

Steven was so moved by Betsy's gesture, he was speechless. This changed everything.

He finally turned to Cara, who was sitting quietly next to him. "I—I—" he stammered.

"I know, Steve. It's time to begin again. And if you still want me, I'm here for you."

Steven took Cara in his arms. "Yes, yes, of course I want you." He placed a soft kiss on Cara's lips. Steven's heart swelled with happiness, and he felt as if Tricia were smiling down on them.

Sixteen

The noise in the Sweet Valley High cafeteria was deafening, and the table where Elizabeth was seated was among the loudest. Winston Egbert was standing books on end next to one another and letting them fall like dominoes. Bruce Patman and Charlie Markus, one of his tennis teammates, were fiercely debating the merits of different tennis players. Elizabeth was trying to explain a math problem to Enid, and Lila Fowler and Sandy Bacon were teasing Jessica. They both found it hilarious that after months of Jessica's plotting ways to get her brother and Cara Walker together, it took Betsy Martin, of all people, to make the two a couple. But Jessica insisted that she had done all the *real* work in setting up the relationship. Betsy was getting the credit just for putting on some finishing touches.

Only Emily Mayer sat quietly, her eyes downcast. Elizabeth glanced up at her once or twice with a worried look. Jessica had told her about Emily's problems at home, and the poor girl looked as if she was at the breaking point.

"Hey, Emily," Guy Chesney called out from the other end of the table, "can The Droids practice at your house tonight?"

"I . . . I don't think so," she stammered. Then she got up suddenly, gathered her books, and left the table in a rush.

Elizabeth looked after her. "Enid, I think you've got it now. I'll be right back." She followed Emily out of the cafeteria and into the ladies' room across the hall.

Emily was standing alone by the sink, sobbing into a paper towel. Elizabeth walked up to her. "Emily?" she said tentatively.

Emily looked up, startled. "Elizabeth. I just want to be alone right now."

"What's wrong? Is there anything I can do to help?"

Emily turned away. "Nobody can help. My own father wants to send me away from Sweet Valley!"

"Oh, Emily, I'm sure you're wrong."

"No way. I heard him talking to my stepmother. He said it was time to think about sending me to boarding school. And of course Karen agreed."

"Maybe they think you're unhappy at home," Elizabeth said with concern.

"It's more like they're unhappy having me around," Emily said bitterly. Then her voice broke. "Oh, Elizabeth, what am I going to do? I love Sweet Valley. I don't ever want to leave!"

Will Emily be forced to go to boarding school? Find out in Sweet Valley High #25, NOWHERE TO RUN, coming next month.

Special Offer
Buy a Bantam Book
for only 50¢.

Now you can order the exciting books you've been wanting to read straight from Bantam's latest listing of hundreds of titles. *And* this special offer gives you the opportunity to purchase a Bantam book for only 50¢. Here's how:

By ordering any five books at the regular price per order, you can also choose any other single book listed (up to $4.95 value) for only 50¢. Some restrictions do apply, so for further details send for Bantam's listing of titles today.

Just send us your name and address and we'll send you Bantam Book's SHOP AT HOME CATALOG!